Dreaming of Mistletoe

Dianna Houx

Contents

Chapter 1

Tess stepped off the train, her unkempt hair whipping in the winter wind. Was it possible it was colder here than in Chicago? Usually it was the other way around, but she supposed it could just be her anticipation of a frosty reception once she reached home causing her to feel that way. The thought of 'home' sent a shiver down her spine. After everything she'd been through, that was no longer a word that held meaning for her.

"Hey lady, keep it moving will ya!" a man yelled from behind her.

Startled, she gave herself a mental shake, then began to walk toward the station exit. "Sorry," she called over her shoulder.

Outside, she pulled out her phone and looked up the make and model of her Uber, checking the cars lined up against the curb for matching plates.

"Over here," a man said, signaling to her.

She double-checked the information, tossed her bags in the trunk, then got in the backseat behind him.

"It says here you're going to... Winterwood?" he asked, his brow raised as he looked at her through the rearview mirror.

"Is that a problem?" she asked, her brow mimicking his. Yes, Winterwood was a small town, and no, people don't usually take Ubers there, but it's not like the guy didn't know what he was signing up for when he accepted the job.

He shook his head. "No problem at all, just wanted to make sure you hadn't picked that town by mistake."

Oh, it was a mistake alright, but one borne of necessity. What else can you do when your entire life implodes overnight but go home and beg your family for mercy?

She checked her messages again—still nothing. Not one single 'checking on you' or 'how you holding up' text from one single person who claimed to be her friend. It's not like they weren't one hundred percent aware of her situation—she'd only been calling and texting them for the last twenty-four hours.

Man, she was tired. Not 'traveling-all-night-with-no-sleep' tired, no, it was so much more than that. The kind of tired you get when you're weary to the bone, and no amount of rest will fix it. She leaned her head back against the seat rest and closed her eyes for just a moment...

"We're almost there," her driver announced.

Tess opened her eyes and looked out the window; one more left turn and she would officially be back in Winterwood. As the old buildings on Main Street came into view, the feeling she was making a big mistake by coming back here intensified—or maybe that was just her anxiety talking. After all, how many people were enthusiastic about going home with their tail tucked between their legs after losing everything? Not to mention, she hadn't exactly left on good terms... it would serve her right if her aunt and uncle slammed the door in her face.

The Uber driver pulled up in front of Bea's Bakery and put the car in park. "We're here," he announced, popping the trunk with the push of a button. "Merry Christmas!"

Now that she was officially here, she had to fight the urge to tell the driver to get back on the road and take her... anywhere but here. Unfortunately, she'd spent all the money she had on the train ticket and car ride that she simply did not have the means to go anywhere else. So, with her tail firmly planted between her legs, she got out of the car, grabbed what was left of her meager belongings from the trunk, and let herself into her aunt's store.

Once inside, she took a deep breath, her stomach rumbling as the scent of gingerbread mixed with chocolate washed over her. She closed her eyes as memories from her childhood flashed through her mind. How many times had she stood in this very spot begging for a cookie or other sweet treat?

"Why, Teresa Joy, are my eyes deceiving me, or is that really you?"

Tess opened her eyes at the sound of her Aunt Bea's voice. "It's me," she said softly. "But I go by Tess now."

Bea nodded, her head tilted as she studied her niece. "You look like something the cat dragged in," she said in concern. "Take a seat over there," she added, pointing to a table in the corner by the window. "I'll be right back."

She did as she was told, wincing when she saw her reflection in the glass. Her long, straight brown hair hung in limp, greasy strands down her back, her bangs practically plastered to her forehead. The only sign of makeup were the black smudges under her eyes from her mascara, along with a few tear-stained streaks down her cheeks. Bea was right—she did look like something the cat had dragged in.

While she waited, she did her best to look past her reflection to the activity across the street. A group was decorating the outside of the bar, the empty building beside it, and the newspaper office. She searched the faces for someone familiar but found none. How was it possible to grow up in a town this size and not know a single person in a large group? Apparently, some things had changed in the years since she'd left.

A plate of warm cinnamon rolls and a steaming cup of coffee materialized in front of her, those pesky tears threatening to make another grand appearance as she looked up in time to see her aunt pull out the chair opposite her.

"I don't deserve your kindness," Tess told her as she stuffed the cinnamon roll into her mouth.

"Nonsense," Bea replied, waving her off. "You're family, darlin'. Ain't nothing ever gonna change that."

How she could say that was anyone's guess. Had Aunt Bea forgotten how horrible she'd been? Because the memory was still fresh in Tess's mind all these years later. She'd just received her employment package from the marketing firm in Chicago. After four rounds of interviews, they hired her: Tess from middle-of-nowhere Winterwood. Visions of her fist-pumping as she danced and yelled in excitement flashed before her like a scene from a movie. If that wasn't embarrassing enough, the next scene was of her coming here, to this very bakery, and yelling out: 'I did it! I'm the first person in our family to actually make something of herself!' Yeah, she'd actually had the nerve to say that to the woman who'd run a successful bakery for decades. To the uncle who'd dedicated his whole life to farming. The word karma came to mind, and this was her comeuppance.

"Want to tell me what happened?" Bea asked, her hands wrapping around her coffee cup as she waited.

The last thing Tess wanted was to tell her what happened, but what choice did she have? "Well, it's like this," she began, unsure of how to begin her tale of woe. "I woke up yesterday morning thinking I was the luckiest woman alive. I had my dream job, lived in an awesome apartment with an amazing view of the skyline, and thought I met my soulmate," she said, choking on the last word.

Bea reached across the table and squeezed her hand, her face a mask of sympathy. "I take it this story doesn't have a happy ending," she drawled.

Tess shook her head. "When I got to work, I was immediately ushered into my boss's office." She wiped her eyes with a napkin. "Even though our company had record profits this year, they were downsizing due to inflation or whatever," she said, her eyes rolling as anger coursed through her at the injustice. "I begged my boss—and I mean literally begged him—to at least let me stay till the end of the year. It's the holidays; no one hires during the holidays! But no, he claimed there was nothing he could do, so I was forced to suffer the humiliation of being led out by security."

She took a deep breath and tried to calm the tears that were now flowing due to frustration. "I spent the rest of the day at a café, sending my résumé to every company with a job opening in a hundred-mile radius."

"Oh, honey," Bea said, handing her more napkins. "I'm so sorry to hear this, but I have no doubt you'll find another job soon."

The rational part of her knew her aunt was trying to be supportive; the emotional part wanted to scream. What did Bea know about the job market? She hasn't job-hunted since Reagan was in office. "That's not all," she replied, her chin quivering. "When I got home, there was an eviction notice on the door. Apparently, my roommate had been pocketing the rent, utility, and insurance money I'd been giving her the last three months, and had moved out while I was at the coffee shop." Tess still couldn't process what had happened. Hannah had been her best friend and roommate for years. How do you claim to be someone's friend and do something like that to them? "She took everything but my clothes."

Bea's mouth dropped open. "I—um."

Watching her usually calm and collected aunt struggle to find words brought Tess a strange sense of peace. Bea always had an answer to everything; it was nice to see her fumble for once.

"Oh, and don't forget about 'Mr. Soulmate,'" Tess said sarcastically. "He worked in a different department from me, and once he found out I'd been unceremoniously kicked to the curb, he ghosted me!" She blinked back tears; this one had actually hurt the worst. They'd only dated for a few months but had already discussed the future and the possibility of marrying one day. The fact he didn't even feel the need to say goodbye had felt like a punch to the gut.

"Honey," Bea began, her eyes wide from all the revelations.

Tess cut her off. "There's nothing to say," she said, in no mood for more platitudes. "I know I have no right to ask this after the way I treated you before I left, but I'm broke, jobless, and homeless. I gave the Uber driver who brought me here the last cent I had and literally have nowhere else to go. I'm willing to work for room and board. Wherever you need me. Here at the bakery, at the farm helping Uncle Junior—whatever it takes."

Bea looked taken aback by her bluntness. "You don't have savings?"

"No," Tess shook her head. "I'd just given all the money I'd saved to my roommate for our renter's insurance. Which, according to her socials, she is using to fund a month-long trip to Sydney with her boyfriend and his family," she said, her words dripping with venom and bitterness. "The only good thing to have come out of all of this was it was her name on the lease and not mine. Otherwise, I'd still be on the hook for money I'd already paid."

"That poor landlord," Bea said, shaking her head.

Tess snorted. "Yes of course, the landlord is the one we should feel sorry for," she said sarcastically. "I'm sure he'll survive. I can't say the same about me, can I?"

"This is just a temporary phase," Bea assured her. "You're still young, honey. There's plenty of time to land back on your feet."

Easy for her to say—she wasn't the one begging her relatives for a roof over her head. Why do people always assume age plays a part in 'landing on one's feet'? Sure, she may have more time until retirement, but nothing is nothing regardless of age. If she wasn't lucky enough to have family, who knows what would happen to her.

"So can I stay with you?" she asked, exhaustion taking hold now that she'd spilled her guts.

"Of course," Bea said without hesitation. "Right now I think you should go back to the farm, take a long hot shower, then take a nap. We can discuss work once you've had a chance to rest and recover from the shock you've received."

Tess wanted to protest, *should* protest, but a hot shower and a warm bed sounded so heavenly she didn't have it in her. "Thank you," she said instead. "Unfortunately, I don't have a way out to the farm."

"That's right, you said you gave your last dollar to the Uber driver," Bea said, nodding as she remembered that part of the story. "No matter, I'll run you out there real quick."

"Thank you," Tess whispered, her tears streaming in earnest. She didn't deserve her aunt's kindness, but she was so grateful for it, words could not express her gratitude.

As she climbed into the front seat, a weight lifted from her shoulders. There was a lot of work ahead, but for now, she was warm, she was safe, and she had a place to stay. That alone felt like a Christmas miracle.

Chapter 2

Tess awoke to the scent of coffee and bacon, but it wasn't the scents that stirred her—it was the hushed voices that accompanied them, the sound of which carried much farther than she suspected their speakers knew. As quietly as possible, she slipped from beneath the covers, quickly wrapped her robe around her, and then crept toward the kitchen, careful to stay hidden in the shadows.

"I'm just saying, I don't know why she came back here," Junior told Bea. "Town this size has almost zero job opportunities. What's she going to do, cashier at the grocery store?"

"If that's what she has to do," Bea replied. "Besides, it's only temporary. I'm sure once she gets another job, she'll be out of here in a flash."

The sound of utensils scraping plates caught her attention. Her uncle was likely finishing up breakfast. Should she hurry to dress and offer to go with him? Or stay and see if they say anything else? She knew she should pick option one, but her curiosity kept her feet firmly planted.

"I don't know, Bea," Junior continued. "I love Teresa, but are we doing the right thing by letting her move back here? I don't want to enable irresponsible behavior."

The urge to scream reared its head once more. What had she done that could possibly be deemed irresponsible? Okay, sure, giving her rent money to her roommate instead of handing it to the landlord directly could be considered a no-no, but she'd had zero issues for years. Besides that, how could it possibly be her fault her company laid her off?

"It wasn't her fault," Bea replied. "I know you're still hurt over the way she left, but we can't let our feelings cloud our judgment. Teresa needs help, and we're going to give it to her."

"You have a heart of gold, darlin'," Junior told her. "I just hope that girl appreciates it this time. You cried for weeks after she left—I don't want to see you go through that again."

Tess's eyes widened at her uncle's words. Had she really behaved badly enough to make her aunt cry? She tried to picture the last time she'd seen them:

The sun had just risen on a hot June morning, yet Tess had been so excited to leave her car was already packed and ready to go. It would take eight hours to drive to Chicago, and she couldn't wait to get there and start her new life.

She grimaced as the memory flashed before her eyes.

"Goodbye, Uncle Junior," she'd said, flinging her arms around his neck.

"Goodbye, sweetheart," he replied. "Don't be a stranger!"

"I doubt I'll have time to get back here for at least a couple of years," she told him. "But maybe you guys could come visit me?" She looked around the farm. "Never mind, that's too big of an ask. Y'all haven't left Winterwood in so long you'd probably get lost and I'd have to send a search party!"

Tess smacked her forehead with her palm. Had she really said that? Wow, she was a jerk.

"Goodbye, Aunt Bea," she said, hugging her next. "I'll make sure to call you once I get there and tell you all about the things you're missing out on!"

A groan escaped, and she quickly covered her mouth with her hand. She'd said the words teasingly, but they all knew she meant them. Tess had made it clear to everyone she knew she hated living in a small town and believed that everyone who stayed did so because they weren't capable of making something of themselves and getting out. She would be different. She would be successful. She literally insulted everyone she knew and loved. This really was karma, and she really did deserve every bit of it.

The sound of the back door slamming shut jolted her back to the present. She'd missed her chance to offer to help her uncle, but given his current mood, maybe that was for the best. Aunt Bea was more likely to be receptive to her help anyway—better to start with her.

Tess walked into the kitchen and let out a yawn, stretching her arms dramatically above her head. "Something sure smells good in here," she said cheerfully. She made a beeline to the sink, grabbed some soap and a sponge, and began to wash the dishes. "Is it almost time to head to the bakery? I can be ready to go in about five minutes."

Bea gave her an assessing look over the rim of her coffee cup. "Today is Sunday, dear," she replied. "The bakery has always been closed on Sundays."

Her tone was almost accusatory, as if she were offended Tess had forgotten that particular detail.

Tess looked over her shoulder, her eyes wide in surprise. "Is it really Sunday? I could have sworn it was Monday." She shook her head and went back to the dishes. "In that case, what would you like me to do today?"

"We should start with some breakfast," Bea said, turning to face the stove. "Eggs and bacon okay?"

Greasy eggs and bacon were the last things Tess wanted. Once she moved, she'd done a complete overhaul of her diet and now preferred oatmeal and fruit, but she was too afraid to rock the boat, so she smiled and nodded instead. She needed a job, a place to live, and money to buy her own food, and she needed it STAT!

"After church, some of the townsfolk plan to work on setting up more decorations," Bea said as she cracked eggs into the skillet. "I think it might do you some good to help out. You can catch up with some of your old friends... who knows, it might help you get into the holiday spirit!"

The last thing Tess cared about was the 'holiday spirit' when her entire life was now the living embodiment of a cesspool. Why her aunt thought otherwise was a mystery, but again, she couldn't afford to rock the boat. "I'd be happy to help," she said through gritted teeth. Thankfully, her back was to her aunt so she couldn't see the pained expression on her face.

"Great!" Bea exclaimed. She put a plate full of food on the counter. "Eat your breakfast while it's hot. I'll let you know when it's time to go."

As Tess took her seat, Bea spun on her heel and left, leaving Tess to eat alone. She took a few bites, then quickly scraped what was left into the garbage disposal and finished the dishes. This was her life now—she had best get used to it.

***

Tess watched with interest as Bea pulled into the parking lot of a neighboring church. "What happened to the old church? Was there some sort of scandal?" It was hard to imagine a scandal big enough to cause Bea to change churches; after all, she'd been attending the old one for decades. Whatever happened, it must be good!

"No, nothing like that. The church was damaged in a recent storm, so it's currently closed for repairs," Bea explained. "Pastor Steve graciously invited us all to come here in the meantime."

That was disappointing. Nothing good ever happened in these small towns. "Is Pastor Allen still pastor of your church?" Tess asked as Bea parked.

Bea nodded. "And he's still the mayor. But he's currently out of town dealing with personal business."

"It sounds like not much has changed since I left," Tess mused, not at all surprised by the news. Lack of change was one of the things she'd hated most. Everything was always the same. Same mayor, same town council, same people working at the store, the bank, the library, the gas station, and on and on. By the time she was in high school, every day had begun to feel like that movie *Groundhog Day*.

"Not everything is the same," Bea pointed out. "Look around—when was the last time you saw the town come together like this?" she said, pointing to all the decorations.

That was a fair point. "What's the deal with that, anyway?" She looped her arm with her aunt's and followed her down the path to the church.

"It's a long story, but a dear friend asked the town for help last Christmas, and we all just sort of came together and helped her out. We loved it so much, we decided to make it a new tradition." Bea gave her a pointed look. "I'm pretty sure you went to school with her—do you remember Grace Parker?"

The name didn't ring a bell, so Tess searched her memory. "Was she the shy bookworm? Red hair? Kept to herself?"

"That's her right there," Bea said, pointing to a woman approaching the church from the opposite side.

Tess turned toward the woman, who was in fact the shy bookworm. That also wasn't a surprise, but what was a surprise was the handsome cowboy Grace was clinging to. "Wait a minute, is that Cole Reed?" If Tess had known that man still lived here, she might not have been so quick to leave.

Bea chuckled. "Guess that's one more thing that's changed," she teased. "Cole is Grace's fiancé."

A pang of jealousy hit her square in the face. Grace was one of the ones who stayed behind, yet here she was, engaged to every schoolgirl's crush. On top of that, she had apparently become the town sweetheart. Was it too late to catch the next bus out of town? Oh, that's right—no buses came to this town. Perfect. She was stuck.

To her horror, Bea led them over to the couple.

"Hey Grace, Cole," Bea said. "I'd like you to meet my niece, Tess, though you may already know each other."

Tess groaned inwardly, yet dutifully shook hands with both of them. She watched Grace closely, waiting for her to step closer to Cole or make some other outward claim toward him, but she did neither of those things. Instead, she smiled warmly at her, which only made Tess feel worse. Apparently, she was now such a loser, women didn't consider her a threat to their relationships.

"I remember you," Grace said sweetly. "You were a couple years ahead of me, but I remember watching you cheer at the football games!"

"How are your parents?" Cole asked. "I heard they sold the farm and moved to Florida a couple years ago."

Her shoulders tensed at the reminder. "Actually, they moved while I was still in high school," she replied, her smile now forced. "We haven't really kept in touch, but I'm sure they're doing well."

"Oh," Cole said, exchanging an awkward glance with Grace. "Time has really gotten away from me..."

"That's what happens when all you do is work," Grace teased. She shivered. "We should get inside before we turn into popsicles!"

Tess watched them as they walked away, their footsteps in sync as they talked with their heads close together. Had she and her ex ever been that close? She called him her soulmate, yet the man ghosted her the second something bad happened. She barely knew Cole, but from what little she'd just witnessed, he would never dream of doing that to Grace. Some women had all the luck.

Once they were settled into a pew, Tess looked around at all the familiar and not-so-familiar faces. Maybe more had changed than she thought. As Pastor Steve approached the podium, she studied him, surprised to see he was younger than she expected. Were pastors getting younger? Or was she now so old ten to fifteen years no longer felt like such a huge age gap? That was a sobering thought. She really needed to get out of here—her mental health depended on it.

Chapter 3

Church was finally over, and Tess was itching to get out of there. She'd spent the entire time studying the faces in the crowd, and to her immense horror, she recognized way too many of them. It was only a matter of time before someone asked why she was back, and that was the absolute last question on earth she wanted to answer. Her aunt, however, did not appear to share her desire, since she seemed determined to speak to every last person in attendance. Too bad Tess couldn't leave without her...

"Well hello there," Pastor Steve called out as Tess passed by him. "I noticed you sitting with Bea and Junior. Are you visiting for the holidays?"

She stopped to shake his hand, grateful for the excuse he'd just given her. "Yep! I thought it would be nice to spend some time with my aunt and uncle," she said, feigning a warm smile. "My name is Tess, by the way." She bit back a grimace, ashamed to not only be lying in church but to the Pastor as well. Karma was really going to come for her now, and she had a feeling it wasn't going to be pretty.

"It's nice to meet you, Tess," he said, giving her hand another shake. "I'm Pastor Steve, though I'm sure you already know that!"

The woman behind her began to 'tut,' signaling it was time to move on.

"Well, I'm sure your aunt and uncle are thrilled to have you here, for however long you're with us," he said.

Thankfully, he turned his attention to the woman behind her, sparing Tess the awkwardness of responding—especially since it was also a lie, if Junior and Bea's discussion that morning was any indication. She continued outside, her sole mission to get to the car before someone else recognized her.

"Teresa? Is that you?"

Of course lady luck was not on her side. Tess stopped and turned to see who had called out to her, groaning inwardly when two of her fellow cheerleaders, Cassie and Evie, along with two attractive men, came into view. She pasted on her best fake smile and squealed along with them as they took turns hugging.

"Wow, it's been ages since we saw you last," Evie said, holding Tess at arm's length so she could give her an appraising look. "You look amazing! City life must really agree with you!"

Tess laughed uncomfortably. "It's been great!" she replied enthusiastically, which wasn't exactly a lie. Until last Friday, things actually had been great. "How about you guys?" she asked as she eyed the men. "What's new with you?"

Evie held out her left hand. "I got married!" she exclaimed. She then turned to the tall man next to her. "This is my husband, Jake!"

"And this is Conor," Cassie said, indicating the man she was holding hands with. "We're not married—"

"—yet!" Conor interrupted as he smiled lovingly at Cassie.

Cassie rolled her eyes but smiled back at him. "We'll see..." she said mysteriously.

"How long are you back for?" Evie asked. "We should get together for lunch sometime."

Oh boy, what was she supposed to say to that? She had no idea how long she would be staying, nor did she have money for luxuries like lunch with friends. "I'll be here through the holidays," Tess said slowly. "How about I check with my aunt and get back to you on lunch?"

Evie gave her a strange look but nodded. "Sounds good. It was nice seeing you again, Teresa!"

The four of them walked off in the direction of the parking lot, Tess booking it in the opposite direction. Somehow she'd managed to avoid any uncomfortable conversations, but she had a feeling that would change soon enough. She finally reached her aunt's car and quickly hopped in the passenger seat. No doubt it would be a long wait, so she settled in, prepared to people-watch as she passed the time.

Sparks of jealousy ignited as she watched; all of them seemed so happy, her misery in stark contrast. She tried to remind herself this was only a temporary setback, not a permanent state of being. But she didn't really know that, did she? There was a very real possibility she could end up stocking shelves at the grocery store for the rest of her life. Tess tried to shake off that thought before depression set in. Things would be okay. They simply had to be.

***

To her immense relief, they'd skipped lunch at Addie's Diner and had eaten leftovers at the farm instead. For a minute, it had almost felt like old times, before she'd stuck her foot in her mouth and offended the people she loved most.

"They're waiting for you back at the church," Junior said, tossing a set of keys on the table in front of Tess. "Since you don't have a car for some reason, you can take my old truck." He wiped his mouth with a napkin, then pushed his chair back. "I need to get back to work."

Tess looked from the keys to her uncle's retreating back. She desperately wanted to call out to him, to apologize, but knew he wasn't ready to hear it. Junior Wilhelm was honest, hardworking, and fair, but once you got on his bad side, it was difficult to get off it.

"Give him time," Bea said, squeezing Tess's hand. She stood and began to clear the plates. "By the way, what *did* happen to your car?"

"I sold it about a month after I moved to Chicago," she replied. When Bea raised her brow, Tess continued to explain. "The apartment I rented was street parking only, and it was such a pain to find a spot. Plus there were all these rules," she waved her hand, "after the third parking ticket, I said forget it and sold the car."

Bea frowned. "But how did you get around?"

"I walked," Tess said with a shrug. "When that wasn't feasible, I ordered an Uber."

"Do you at least still have a driver's license?"

Luckily, she did. She could just imagine how upset her aunt and uncle would be if she had to tell them she'd let her license expire. "Yes, it was either renew it or apply for a government ID, so I renewed it," she replied, grabbing the keys. "I better get over to the church before they start without me."

"Have fun, dear!"

Was this supposed to be fun? Tess had somehow gotten the impression this was more punishment than pleasure, but maybe she'd misread the situation? Or maybe that had simply been her interpretation, since she couldn't imagine a task more tedious and boring than hanging Christmas lights.

Junior's truck was just as she remembered it: old, rusty, and smelled like cow. If she had a handkerchief, she would tie it around her nose and mouth to stop the gagging. Since she didn't, she had to settle for turning the heat on max while rolling down both windows. Not that it mattered—no matter what she did, the smell was there, permeating every inch of her clothing, hair, and nostrils. No doubt about it, when she exited the truck, she too would smell like she'd been out wrastlin' cows in the field.

Ten minutes later, she pulled up to the church—for the second time that day—and exited the truck. As she looked around for a sign of the others, she pulled her hair up into a messy bun and secured it with an old piece of baling twine she'd found in the cab. Spotting a group of people in front of the church, she made her way there.

"Hey everyone," she said, giving them a small wave. "What can I do to help?"

"Is that your truck?" one of the women asked, pointing toward Junior's rust bucket.

Tess nodded, curious as to why she was asking.

"Can you run over to the feed store and grab a couple of square bales of straw?" she asked. "We want the manger scene to be more authentic."

"Um, sure," Tess replied, already turning back toward the truck. From what little she'd seen, the 'manger scene' appeared to be comprised of plastic figures, so 'authentic' was a bit of a reach. But who was she to argue?

The feed store was located across town and took approximately four minutes to reach by truck. Back in Chicago, it would likely be a twenty-minute walk. She pulled up in front and sighed, she really needed to let that go. Reminding herself of how things were was not helpful. Besides that, there was still the possibility she could make it back one day. She'd sent out a ton of résumés before she left; all she needed was one of them to pan out. And a way to get back there... a place to live... money for food and rent... she sighed again. It was hopeless.

She braced herself for the blast of cold, then hopped out of the truck and rushed inside, the familiar shades of beige welcoming her like an old friend—this place hadn't changed one single bit since the last time she was there.

"Can I help you find something?" a voice called from behind the counter.

Tess turned to see who was talking to her, her eyes widening in surprise when she came face-to-face with her old friend. "Austin! You're still working here?" She winced at the tone of her voice, half-accusatory, half-dumbfounded. Could she be any more insulting if she tried?

Austin smiled. "Yep! What brings you back to town, Teresa? I haven't seen you in, oh, three? Four years?"

"Four," Tess said, more for her benefit than his. "It's actually Tess now, and I'm just here visiting my aunt and uncle for the holidays," she replied, once again lying through her teeth. If she didn't get a new job soon, she would have a lot of explaining to do to a lot of people. But she would cross that bridge when she came to it.

He looked at her expectantly.

"Oh, that's right," she said, laughing awkwardly. "I need a couple bales of straw."

"Pull the truck around back and I'll load 'em for you," he drawled. "I'll just go ahead and charge it to Junior's account real quick."

Tess tensed at the mention of money. The lady at the church hadn't said anything about paying for the straw, and she hadn't thought to ask. Uncle Junior might not notice the extra charge, but she wasn't sure about that either. She would just have to remember to talk to him about it later. "Sounds good," Tess replied. "I'll meet you there." She started to walk away, then stopped and turned back to him. “Hey, why isn’t this place decorated? Is old man Williams still too cheap to buy decorations?”

A strange look crossed his face, but he quickly shook it off. “Nah, we’re on the outskirts of town, so we don’t bother with all that,” he explained.

“Oh, come on, not even a tree?” Why she was harassing him about something she found ‘tedious and boring’ was beyond her, but she found herself doing it anyway. Maybe misery loved company?

Austin gave her a look. “No one from the B&B, nor any visitors that come for the festival, are likely to come to the *feed store*,” he drawled.

“But what about your regular customers?” she asked, her brow raised. “Don’t you think they’d enjoy a little holiday spirit?”

“I’ll give it some thought,” he said gruffly.

“Fair enough,” she replied. She drove around back, spotted the straw pile, then pulled up to it. While she waited, her mind wandered to Austin and how sad it was he was still working at the feed store. He’d started when he was sixteen, so that meant he’d worked here now for what, twelve years? Talk about a small-town guy who was going nowhere fast. Even if he did have bulging biceps from years of lifting heavy bags of feed and slinging bales of hay. Or that wavy brown hair that curled at his neck and ears... or those soulful brown eyes that reminded her of a chocolate lab... or that crooked smile...

Snap out of it, she reprimanded herself. The last thing she needed was to fall for the town loser. He probably still made minimum wage and lived with his mom. Not that she was much better—being unemployed and living with her aunt and uncle. But that was obviously temporary. After twelve years, Austin could not say the same. No, it was best not to go down this road. She was just feeling some kind of way after seeing everyone in town paired off earlier. Besides that, for all she knew, Austin had a girlfriend. Or maybe even a wife. Probably some waitress over at Addie's. Yep, nothing to see here, best to keep it moving...

Tess was still chastising herself when Austin finally appeared.

"Sorry about that," he said sheepishly. "Another customer came in right after you left and I had to help her before I could get out here."

"It's okay," Tess replied. She wasn't about to tell him this, but she wouldn't have cared if it took him the rest of the day to get her the straw. The more time she spent here, the less time she'd have to decorate. In fact, she could have loaded the bales herself, should she have been inclined to do so.

Austin lifted a square bale in each hand, then flung them into the bed of the pickup. "Must be nice to have so much time off work," he said casually. "I can't remember the last time I had a week off, much less three."

There was something in his tone, something she couldn't quite place. Did he know? It was possible Junior had been by since she'd been back and told Austin all about her troubles, but she didn't think he would do that. So if that wasn't the cause of his attitude, what was? "I saved up my vacation days so I could take them all at once," she said, wishing that were the truth. She might need to consider making a note of all the lies she was telling to keep them straight. "You know, you could do that too if you got a job somewhere that actually had benefits," she pointed out. "Of course, that might mean you had to leave town..."

He gave a curt nod. "Well, there ya go," he said, waving toward the bed. "I'm open till five if you need anything else." He walked off without looking back, his head down against the cold.

Had he really just dismissed her like that? She might not have bothered to keep in touch these last four years, but they had been friends once upon a time. Did that mean nothing to him? Or was he mad about the benefits comment? What could she say—some people don't like hearing the truth.

Oh well, that just made it easier for her to put all thoughts of him and his muscles aside, although he did look good in that flannel shirt and Carhartt jacket... She shook her head and got back in the truck. Back to work; plastic Mary and Joseph need their straw!

Chapter 4

Tess was up with the roosters this morning. Literally. The roosters on the farm literally woke her up at the crack of dawn, and if there was anything she missed about farm life, it was NOT this.

Still exhausted from spending eight hours decorating the day before, she trudged into the kitchen and made a beeline straight for the coffee pot. Bea's coffee wasn't exactly a 'skinny cinnamon dolce latte,' but the warm brew sure did hit the spot.

"Okay," she said once she'd taken a couple of sips, "what's on the agenda for today?"

Bea looked up from her oatmeal and took in Tess's stringy, mussed hair, her face scrunching in distaste at the smudged mascara Tess hadn't bothered to wash off the night before. "First up is a shower for you, young lady," she said, clucking her tongue. She sniffed the air. "Do I smell cow?"

"Oh, come on," Tess said, rolling her eyes. "You live on a farm with your farmer husband. Surely this isn't the first time someone has smelled like a cow."

"I'm just saying," Bea replied. "Anyway, can you be ready in ten minutes? I need to get to the bakery and could use your help today. My normal helper has been somewhat unreliable these days."

It would have been nice to at least finish her coffee first, but Tess figured there would be plenty of time for that later.

"By the way," she said as she walked out of the room, "I had to charge a couple bales of straw to Uncle Junior's account at the feed store yesterday. I hope that's okay? I wasn't really given another option."

"I'll let him know," Bea said, shooing Tess out the door. "Make sure you wash your hair; I have a reputation to maintain!"

Tess rolled her eyes a second time. In a town like Winterwood, she highly doubted she would be judged on her hair—or that someone would refuse to buy a cookie because she didn't look like she stepped out of a fashion magazine. But whatever, she would do as she was told.

Twenty minutes later, they were on the road, Tess's hair now in a wet French braid. She was probably going to catch her death from the cold, but these days, that seemed preferable to her current circumstances.

"I take it you saw Austin yesterday?" Bea asked, her tone casual, as if she were simply making conversation.

Four years may have passed since she'd last seen her aunt, but Tess was still wise to her gossipy ways. "I did," she said with a shrug. "Guess old man Williams still expects him to work Sundays," she mused. "Kind of sad a grown man like that is still working the same shifts he did as a teenager."

Bea side-eyed her. "Old man Williams sold the feed store to Austin about six years ago."

Tess's head whipped toward her aunt. "That's not possible!" she exclaimed. "I was still living here back then. There's no way he bought the store and didn't tell me!"

"You were at college," Bea reminded her. "You only came back during school breaks, and I'm pretty sure I did tell you about it; you just chose not to listen."

"Fine, maybe you did," Tess agreed. In all likelihood, she probably did. This was exactly the kind of thing her aunt would have loved to gossip about. "I might not have listened to you, but I definitely would have listened to him."

"Maybe he thought you knew and was waiting for you to say something to him," Bea pointed out.

That... made sense. Austin would have assumed Bea told her and would have waited for her to congratulate him. When she didn't, he would have stewed in silence, choosing to assume she didn't care. Men could be so stupid sometimes, but then again, so could she. She smacked her hand against her forehead as their conversation from yesterday replayed in her head. He must think she is incredibly stupid to make comments to him about 'benefits' and 'leaving town' when he's the owner of the whole freaking store! She'd even called him the town loser, though thankfully she hadn't said that part out loud. She really was a jerk. A stuck-up, snotty, classist jerk.

While she lamented all her life choices, Bea pulled into the back of the bakery. "Are you ready to bake till you ache?"

Tess snorted. "As ready as I'll ever be."

***

Six excruciatingly long hours had passed, and Tess was ready to bedazzle 'bake till you ache' on a t-shirt. Never had a phrase been more accurate. She stretched her arms above her head, the movement causing flour to rain from her hands onto her hair. At this point, she actually missed those tedious, overly long weekly meetings she'd been forced to attend—which surprised her. Until today, no longer having to attend those had been the one bright spot of losing her job.

"You know, Austin's single..." Bea said as she weaved her way through the baking racks, a tray of gingerbread cookies in hand.

Despite her best efforts to play it cool, Tess's ears perked up. "What, no one wants to date the feed store owner?" she snarked.

"A little judgmental for someone in your position, don't you think?" Bea shot back, her brow arched as she stared at Tess.

"I don't know why I said that," Tess admitted as a sigh escaped. "I didn't mean it, I just—"

"Can't seem to help yourself?" Bea finished for her.

Tess stared down at her feet and nodded. Guilt washed over her as she squirmed under her aunt's disapproving gaze. "What's wrong with me?" she whispered.

Bea set the tray down, walked over to Tess, then pulled her into a hug. "There's nothing wrong with you; you just seem to have some sort of deep prejudice against this town. Personally, I blame your parents. I think them leaving you here caused some bitterness to take root in your heart."

"I don't know," Tess said again. "I know they thought they were doing what's best for me, and maybe it was for the best. I guess I've always just felt this need to prove my worth, you know? I mean seriously, I was only two years away from graduating. Couldn't they have waited two more years?"

"Have you talked to them about that?" Bea asked as she absentmindedly brushed flour from Tess's hair.

Tess shrugged. "What's the point? They made their choice, and I made mine."

"The point, darlin', is you're old enough now to try to see things from their perspective."

"Is this your way of getting rid of me?" Tess asked, bitterness dripping from each word. When Bea gave her a surprised look, she continued. "I know you and Junior don't want me here, but if you're hoping my parents and I will have some 'magical Christmas reunion' so you can pawn me off on them, it's not going to happen. And if that's my only option, I'll go live on the street."

Bea let go and took a deep breath, her lips tightening in displeasure at Tess's outburst. "Teresa Joy Wilcox, that is enough out of you! I know you're going through a hard time, but that is no excuse to be disrespectful."

"I'm so—" Tess began.

"I don't want to hear it," Bea interrupted. She grabbed a small to-go box, placed a red velvet cupcake with cream cheese frosting in it, then handed it to Tess. "Save your apologies for Austin, and while you're on your way over there, think long and hard about your attitude."

Tess accepted the box, then walked to the back door to grab her coat. It had been a long time since her aunt had given her a stern talking-to. She honestly thought she was past those, but apparently not.

As soon as she stepped outside, a blast of arctic air hit her smack in the face. Snow flurries danced as the wind swirled around, creating a magical scene against the backdrop of the heavily decorated buildings. It was almost as if she'd been transported to Santa's Village. Almost. Once the cold set in, her inner *Grinch* took over, and before long, she was stomping over to the feed store, barely resisting the urge to grab lights off the buildings and tear them down on the way.

"Someone's in a bad mood," Austin said as Tess stormed into the building.

"This is for you," she said, tossing the cupcake box on the counter. "I'm sorry I was a jerk yesterday." She looked around and saw a couple of strangers watching her. "Fine, and today as well."

Austin was quiet for so long, Tess eventually gave up on a response and turned to leave.

"Do you remember that tree in the park we used to meet at back in high school?" he asked quietly.

Tess nodded, a vivid picture forming in her mind.

"Meet me there at six."

She turned to ask why, but he'd already walked off to help one of the customers who'd been watching her, so she did the only thing she could and left. As she walked back to the bakery, she checked her watch and saw she had three hours until it was time to meet him. That meant she had three hours to imagine all the reasons he wanted to speak to her alone—the most likely being he wanted to tell her off where they couldn't be overheard. Which, fair enough, she supposed she deserved it.

"How did it go?" Bea asked when Tess walked inside. She looked her up and down. "I'm guessing not well since you're back so soon."

"He was busy," Tess replied as she stomped the snow off her boots. "But he wants me to meet him at six. Is that okay?"

Bea raised a brow but nodded. "You can take my car, just try to tone down the attitude, okay? That man isn't your enemy any more than your uncle and I are."

Those words gave her pause. Is that really how she saw everyone? As her enemies? She didn't think so, but she didn't blame them for feeling that way. "I really do appreciate you," Tess told Bea. "I know I haven't acted like it, and for that I'm sorry. I'm just so angry, I keep lashing out and saying things I don't mean."

"I know, honey, and I forgive you." She pulled more trays of cookies out of the oven and set them on the cooling racks. "We just need to finish decorating these for the Christmas party tomorrow and we'll be done for the day."

Tess groaned, her back still hurting from the hundreds of cookies she'd already decorated. "I don't know how you've managed to do this for the last forty years and are still able to walk upright. I'm pretty sure I'm going to look like *The Hunchback of Notre Dame* by the time we're done."

"Let's just hope Austin prefers his date to look like Igor from *Frankenstein*," Bea deadpanned.

"It's not a date," Tess said, laughing. "I'm sure he just wants to tell me how awful I am and hopes I leave in a couple of weeks and never come back."

Bea clucked her tongue. "We will see..."

Chapter 5

Six o'clock came faster than expected, and Tess found herself scrambling to get to the meeting place on time. The last thing she wanted was for Austin to think she was standing him up—not that this was a date, just that, well, you know, she'd already made a huge mess of things and didn't want to be seen as a flake on top of it.

Her hair was once again in a wet French braid, and by that, she meant she didn't have time to dry her hair before she braided it. Once again, she was risking illness by going out in the cold with wet hair, and once again, she found she didn't care. All she wanted was to get this over with so she could go back home and go to bed. Although even that held little appeal since she'd be doing the same thing all over again tomorrow.

Once she finally arrived at the park, she had to admit—it did look like a winter wonderland. The townsfolk had done an amazing job with the decorations, and even she was looking forward to the tree lighting ceremony Saturday. It was unlikely to rival the annual Chicago Tree Lighting Ceremony in Millennium Park... but she was sure it will still be nice.

"I was starting to think you weren't coming," Austin called out.

Tess turned toward the sound of his voice, surprised to see him exiting a rather large—and newish—Ford F-350. How on earth could he afford a truck like that? And why did he need a truck that big? Maybe it belonged to the feed store? That would make sense, though she didn't see the name on the side like most stores had.

"Sorry," Tess said lamely. "I'm not used to driving in the snow, so it took longer than expected to get here."

They fell in step beside each other as they walked to the tree, Tess still not sure why he asked to meet here. When they reached the spot, Austin stopped walking and turned to face her.

"We were friends in high school," he said slowly, as if he were still deciding what to say.

"Yes," Tess agreed. "Hopefully we still are."

He gave her a long look but ignored that last part. "I had a crush on you," he told her with all the emotion of a man detailing what he had for supper. "But I knew you would leave the second you had the chance, so I pushed my feelings aside and did my best to move on with my life."

"Why are you telling me this?" Tess whispered, unsure of how to respond. She'd had a crush on him too, but knew he'd never leave here. And she was right—he hadn't.

"I'm telling you this because I want you to know how I feel and why," he explained. "I never wanted to be the guy begging you to stay. I knew you needed to leave, and I respected you too much to stand in your way."

Tess opened her mouth to speak, but he held up his hand to stop her.

"You've never given me the same respect, and you still aren't. You blow back into town—like this force of nature—and then look down upon all of us because we dared to be happy in a life you hate. It's okay that you prefer to live in the city, Tess, but it's also okay that some of us prefer to live here." He reached out and touched the bark of the tree, some of the snow dusting his gloved fingertips. "I'd like to spend time with you while you're here, but not if all you're going to do is make snide comments about me and my choices."

Without thought, her hand reached out to him and touched his arm. "You're right, I've been a terrible friend, and I'm sorry. My aunt thinks it's because of my parents, but in all honesty, I'm pretty sure it's just me. When I look around, all I see are people living these simple lives..."

Austin laughed. "I think what you're trying to say is 'boring' lives."

She considered that. "Yeah, maybe you're right, nothing ever happens here. It's the same thing day after day, you know? I love the excitement of the city; there's always something going on—some new shop to explore, cafe to eat at, event to go to. I just really struggle to understand why no one else feels the way I do. Don't you ever get tired of working every day with nothing to look forward to but more work?"

"There are days when things feel monotonous," he agreed. "I'd be lying if I said there weren't, but can you honestly tell me you never had days like that too? We don't live that far from a city. You can do all the things you talked about anytime you want, then come home to the peace and quiet of country life. It's like having the best of both worlds, if you ask me."

She supposed he was right, she did have days at her old job that felt like they bled into the next one with no end in sight. There were times when she got tired of trying to sleep through endless car alarms, loud music, and sirens. She'd never thought about that before—she just assumed it was the price she had to pay to be where she thought she wanted to be. Still, she wasn't ready to convert to his way of thinking.

"What if we agree to disagree, and I promise not to make any more rude and unnecessary comments?"

It was hard to see his face in the dark, the light from the lampposts barely enough to illuminate the area around them, but she could have sworn he visibly relaxed at her proposal.

"Deal," he said, holding out his hand.

Tess smiled as they shook hands, relieved to have made amends with at least one person she'd offended.

"So what now?" she asked, not quite ready to say goodbye.

Austin grabbed her hand and led her over to the sidewalk. "Now we walk around town and look at all the Christmas lights!" he exclaimed. "Along the way, we'll stop for a bad cup of coffee at the gas station to warm up."

His enthusiasm was infectious, and before long, Tess was oohing and aahing right along with him.

"I can't remember the last time the town decorated for Christmas," she said as they passed her aunt's bakery. "It must have been before we were born." They paused to look at the window display outside Rustic Petals and Posies. "Linda really outdid herself," Tess said as she shivered from the cold.

"True, but she always does," Austin replied. He wrapped his arm around Tess's shoulders and pulled her close. "I better get you that coffee before you turn into a snowman," he said after another moment of watching the lights on the display.

They continued down the street, Tess panicking a little at the thought of having to explain she didn't have money for coffee. When they entered the gas station, Austin made a beeline for the coffee station, Tess reluctantly trailing behind.

"None for me, thanks," she said when he handed her a cup.

"Seriously?" he asked, his brow furrowed in confusion. "But you're freezing."

That was true, but broke trumped freezing, so what was a girl to do? "I can't have caffeine this late or I'll be up all night," she replied. What was one more lie, right?

"Oh." He turned to look at the machines. "How about hot chocolate then?"

"Um, that gives me heartburn," she said, trying not to sound suspicious as she once again declined the cup.

Austin stared at her for a moment. "Why do I get the feeling you're just making up excuses? I know this isn't one of the fancy coffee shops you're used to, but are you seriously too good for gas station coffee?"

She knew she had that coming, but it still hurt—especially since that wasn't the case. Now she would have to lie to get out of her other lies. At this point, she would need a Venn diagram to keep all the lies straight. "It's not that," she protested.

"Then what's the problem?"

"I left my purse in the car..." she explained.

"And?"

Was he really going to make her spell it out? "And I don't have cash on me to pay for it." She left off the 'duh' but was certain from the look on his face he received the message loud and clear.

"I invited you out," he said slowly, as if speaking to a child. "Which means I have every intention of paying for your coffee, okay? So please stop being ridiculous and pour yourself a cup," he said, handing her the empty cup again.

Seeing as how she was now out of excuses, she did as she was told—more grateful than she cared to admit for the warmth that first sip brought. "You sure have become bossy," she said as they made their way to the cash register.

"And you've become stubborn," he shot back. "Oh wait, you've always been like that."

Tess narrowed her eyes at him, then playfully smacked his arm when he broke out in a grin.

When he finished paying, they braced themselves to go back out into the cold. The snow had stopped, but there were at least a couple of inches to trek through, and by this point, Tess's toes were now ice cubes. If she'd been smart, she would have worn snowshoes, but no—she had to be cute with her leather heeled boots. So now her feet were freezing, *and* they ached. To add insult to injury, Austin hadn't even noticed. Not that she was trying to impress him, but still—it would be nice if her suffering wasn't in vain.

"So tell me about Chicago," he said, as he sipped his coffee. "What have I been missing all my life?"

That felt like such a loaded question, she had no idea where to even begin. Should she tell him about the marketing agency she'd poured her heart and soul into for four years before she became another victim of corporate greed? Or about all her great friends who abandoned her in her time of need? Maybe she should tell him about the man she fantasized about marrying... Suddenly, her time in Chicago didn't seem so great after all.

"We both know you don't really care about Chicago," Tess said, doing her best to sound playful. "How about you tell me all the things I've missed since I've been gone? I see a lot of our classmates are either married or engaged. Anyone in particular I should know about?"

Austin thought about that for a minute. "Do you remember Evie's older sister Shelley?"

"I think so," Tess said, trying to remember who she was.

"You won't believe this, but before Evie married Jake, she was engaged to a man named Greg. Greg dumped Evie at the altar—for Shelley!"

Tess gasped. "You're kidding!"

"I wish I was," Austin said, shaking his head. "It was the talk of the town for months!" He took another sip, then tossed his empty cup in the trash can at the park. "Anyway, about a year later, both Shelley and Greg—still married, by the way—have babies with other people."

"You are so lying," Tess accused. "There is no way this happened. It sounds too much like a soap opera!"

Austin snorted. "I'm not done," he laughed. "Shelley and Greg—who have now split up—teamed up to sabotage Evie and Jake's wedding!"

"If this is true, all I can say is poor Evie!"

He held three fingers up. "Scout's honor!"

Tess shook her head in bewilderment. "Man, I really missed out on this circus. What happened after that?"

"Shelley decided to become a social media star, and last I heard was out in Hollywood trying to make it as a stuntwoman."

"Okay, now I know you're lying," she teased.

"Look, I'll prove it to you," he said, pulling out his phone. He fiddled around with it for a minute, then held it up so Tess could see the screen.

They must have watched at least a dozen videos of Shelley in a wedding dress doing one ridiculous stunt after another. Tess was laughing so hard by the time he showed her the last one, her breaths were coming in short gasps as she dried tears from her eyes.

"And you thought nothing exciting happened in Winterwood," Austin said in mock indignation.

When she could breathe again, they resumed walking, their speed slowing down as they neared their vehicles.

"You got me," she finally said. "Things have definitely become more interesting since I left." She paused for a minute. "Wait a minute, that almost sounds like an insult!"

"You said it, not me," Austin said playfully. When they reached her aunt's car, he waited patiently for her to fish the keys out of her coat pocket. "I had a lot of fun with you tonight," he said, his mood turning from playful to somber.

"I did too," Tess replied, unsure of how to say goodbye without making things awkward. Should she hug him? Shake his hand? Wave? "You know, you really should put a tree up at the store," she told him. "I could always help, you know. I've been forced to do so much decorating, I'm practically an expert now!"

Austin snorted. "You've been home for all of what, three days? How much decorating could you have done in that amount of time?"

"You doubt my skills?" she said in mock indignation. "I'll have you know I decorated at least three hundred gingerbread cookies today, and I have the back pain to prove it!"

"So you plan to decorate the tree with cookies?" When she narrowed her eyes at him, he broke out into a grin. "I'm just giving you a hard time," he said with a laugh. "If you really want to put up a tree, I'll take you out to the tree farm tomorrow after work, okay?"

Is that really what she wanted? Why was she pushing so hard on this? It made absolutely no difference to her if the feed store had a tree or not, and yet, she couldn't seem to let it go. At least it would give her something to do other than sit at home worrying over her future. "That sounds good to me," she replied. "So, I guess I'll see you tomorrow?"

Austin nodded, his hands moving to his pockets as he searched for his keys. "Yep. I'll pick you up at six, unless you want to go a little earlier and grab a pizza on the way there? I know I won't have time for dinner, and I'm usually starving by the time I get off work."

"Yeah, just text me when you're ready." They exchanged phone numbers so they could contact each other.

"Well, goodnight," Austin said. He gave her a half wave, then pivoted on his heel and speed-walked to his truck.

"Goodnight," Tess repeated, more to herself than to him. She got in the car, anxious to get out of the cold and into the heat. Tonight had been fun, but it had also reaffirmed her belief that there was no place for her here. Although, if that were true, why was she already looking forward to tomorrow?

Chapter 6

Tess walked into the kitchen the next morning, and by walked, she meant trudged. Or maybe staggered was a better word? Perhaps lumbered? Shuffled? Whatever it was, it felt like she was wading through molasses, every inch of her body hurting in ways she never knew possible. Worse than that, she discovered soon after she got home last night that caffeine late at night actually did make it difficult for her to sleep. On the one hand, that was one less lie she'd have to keep up with; on the other, she spent the night tossing and turning and now felt like death warmed over. It was going to be a long day.

"How did it go with Austin?"

She groaned in response. Of course her aunt would ask her that first thing when she walked in the door. Didn't she know the golden rule? Don't ask people questions until they've had at least one cup of coffee!

"It went fine," she replied after she'd taken her first sip.

Bea looked at her expectantly. "That's all you have to say?"

"What else do you want to know?" Tess asked, not at all awake enough to have this conversation.

"For starters, is there going to be a second date?"

Tess almost spit out her coffee. "There hasn't been a first date!" she exclaimed. "It was just as I thought it would be. Austin was mad at me over my crappy attitude and wanted me to know about it. Once we cleared the air, we walked around to look at the Christmas decorations, and then we went home. Separately," she added, just in case her aunt got some ideas.

"Hmmph," Bea said, rolling her eyes. "You guys are boring."

"Aunt Bea!"

"Oh, don't get your panties in a wad, I'm just teasing you," Bea said. She patted the chair next to her. "We need to have a talk."

That sounded ominous. Tess slowly approached the table, her adrenaline kicking into overdrive. They'd decided to kick her out after all, hadn't they? What would she do? Where would she go?

"L-look, I—I know I've been a terrible niece, but please don't do this," Tess begged.

Bea gave her a strange look. "What does you being terrible have to do with me retiring?"

Tess blinked several times, unable to process what she just heard. "What do you mean? Retiring from what?"

"Are you okay, dear?" Bea asked, reaching over to feel Tess's forehead with the back of her hand. When she seemed convinced Tess wasn't running a fever, she pulled her hand back and gave her an assessing look. "You do look pretty rough. Maybe now isn't the time..."

"The time for what?" Tess said in exasperation. "Can you please tell me what's going on? My anxiety can't handle the suspense!"

"I'm retiring from the bakery," Bea stated matter-of-factly.

That was not at all what Tess had been expecting. In fact, it wasn't even in the realm of possibilities. "Why?" she asked, growing alarmed. "Are *you* sick? Is Uncle Junior?"

Bea shook her head. "Thankfully, no, but we are getting up there, darlin'. After four decades, these old bones are tired and ready to move on to something else."

"Wow," Tess said, too stunned to say much else.

"You coming back here now, of all times, made me wonder if this is fate," Bea said slowly, as if she were talking it through for the first time. "You need a job... I plan to retire..."

It was obvious Bea was trying to say something, but Tess was having a hard time following along. She really should have been allowed to drink her coffee before this bomb was dropped on her. "Are you trying to say you want me to take over the bakery?" Tess asked, certain she was wrong and any minute her aunt would burst out laughing at such an absurd idea.

"I think you'd be the perfect replacement!" Bea said enthusiastically. "Think about it. You spent years working with me throughout high school. You know all my recipes, have a natural talent at baking, and are well known and liked throughout the community!"

That last part was currently up for debate, but she did at least know all the recipes. If she were honest, this would solve a lot of her problems—specifically the one where she needed a job. The only problem was she hated baking. Like, really hated it. Yesterday had been a stark reminder of all the reasons why: the early mornings, long hours bent over counters, lifting and muscling around heavy sacks of flour or sugar. No, it simply was not for her.

"What about Jenny?" Tess asked, desperate to buy time so she could think of a way to let her aunt down without looking like a jerk. Again.

Bea sighed. "You know I love Jenny. She's an amazing assistant, but she doesn't have what it takes to run a business."

"And I do?" Tess asked in surprise. She'd never seen herself as the entrepreneurial type; it was too much responsibility. Although the thought of not getting fired again did hold some appeal...

"Of course you do!" Bea replied. "You've always been good at the business side of things." She studied Tess for a moment. "But this isn't what your heart wants, is it?"

Would it be wrong to say no? Could beggars really be choosers at a time like this? More importantly, could she really bear to disappoint her aunt again after everything she'd done for her? "Is there anyone else you think would be a better fit?" Tess asked hopefully. If Bea said no, she would agree, but if she said yes...

"There is someone," Bea said cryptically. "In fact, we've already had a conversation about it."

"Then wouldn't it be cruel for me to swoop in and steal it out from under her?"

Bea surprised them both by laughing. "Okay, sweetheart, I understand. I just thought I should talk to you first, just in case."

Tess reached out and grabbed Bea's hand. "Thank you," she said sincerely. "I am honored you thought of me, and sincerely wish I could say yes—"

"But like I said, your heart isn't in it," Bea finished for her.

"No, it isn't." Tess shook her head sadly. Life would be so much easier if she could accept the offer. It would also be so much easier to explain why she was still here after the holidays were over, which triggered a horrifying thought. "Do you think the new owner will let me stay until I find a new job?"

"I have no doubt she will," Bea said. She stood up and walked her dishes over to the sink. "Especially if things continue with Jenny the way they are."

Tess didn't like the sound of that either. The last thing she wanted—or needed—was to be in the middle of someone else's drama. She had enough of her own, thank you very much!

As if sensing her unease, Bea waved her hand dismissively. "We can worry about all this later. For now, we have cookies to bake!"

"More cookies?" Tess groaned. "How many more do you need?"

"Oh, at least another ten dozen," she said with a laugh.

"I'm going to need a lot more coffee."

***

The day passed slowly as Tess counted down the minutes until it was time to go out with Austin. She was looking forward to this way more than someone in her position should be. In fact, she'd had to remind herself multiple times this wasn't a date—it was just two friends hanging out for an evening, just like they used to back in their high school days. It didn't help that Bea kept making little comments about their 'date' and how nice it was the two of them were finally getting together.

Ding

She wiped her hands on a damp towel and checked her phone.

Hey Tess, it's Austin, can you be ready by 5:15?

"Ooh, is that a message from Austin?" Bea asked as she walked by. "Make sure you say 'yes' to whatever he asks!"

Tess rolled her eyes. "What if he asks me to run away to Vegas and get married by an Elvis impersonator?"

Bea arched her brow. "Then I expect you to let me and Junior know the time and date so we can be the witnesses," she deadpanned. "We could use a vacation, you know."

"You are incorrigible!" Tess tried to keep a straight face, but failed miserably when her aunt smiled sweetly at her.

She turned her attention back to her phone. "Guess that means I *can* be ready at 5:15," she muttered.

I'll be ready. Pick me up at the bakery?

Three little dots immediately appeared, followed by the thumbs-up emoji. She checked her watch: 3:30. An hour and forty-five minutes to go—however would she pass the time? Oh, that's right—she still had at least two dozen cookies to ice. At least these were sugar cookies. It was kind of fun to let her inner child loose with the sprinkles.

An hour had passed when Bea walked by again. "Maybe you should go home and change into something... not covered in frosting," she suggested.

"Are you sure?" Tess asked innocently. "I thought men liked a woman who smelled like eau de bakery," she said with an exaggerated fake French accent.

Bea pursed her lips. "I suppose you're right, though it would be better if you looked a little less frumpy. You could always run down to Chrissy's Boutique and get a new shirt."

"I don't have the money for that," Tess reminded her. "Besides that, Austin's also coming from work, so he'll likely be wearing a flannel shirt and smell like hay. Why aren't you over there telling *him* to freshen up for *me*?"

"Some women like the lumberjack look," she said with a shrug. "Anyway, I'll give you money for some new clothes," she said, grabbing her purse.

Tess shook her head. "Honestly, that isn't necessary. All we're doing is putting up a Christmas tree, so there's no need to dress up. And for the umpteenth time, this isn't a date!"

Bea put her wallet back in her purse and sighed. "Fine, have it your way. All I'm saying is it never hurt to look one's best."

While she normally agreed with that, Tess had already tried that last night, and it got her nothing but sore feet.

No, this time she was going for comfort. She checked her watch again—forty-five minutes to go. That should give her just enough time to finish the rest of the cookies.

Chapter 7

Austin was waiting out front, his big truck taking up two parking spaces. As she hauled herself up onto the passenger seat, memories of doing this very thing in high school flooded her mind. His truck had been much smaller then, but she'd still gotten a thrill out of riding shotgun.

Once inside, she smiled nervously, taking in his predicted flannel shirt, jeans, and Carhartt. Thank goodness she hadn't listened to her aunt and bought a new outfit; she would have looked foolishly out of place next to him. Plus, he might have gotten the wrong idea—or worse—thought she had the wrong idea.

"Ready to go to Lyle's?" Austin asked. He put the truck in drive, then slowly pulled out onto the street.

The mention of Lyle's Tree Farm dragged her back to the present. "Lyle's still running the tree farm?" she asked in surprise. "I thought he was old back when we were kids!"

"Actually, it's Lyle Jr. now," Austin informed her. "Lyle Sr. retired a few years ago after he had a stroke while out chopping down trees."

"That's so sad," Tess replied, her heart aching for the family. A part of her had always feared she'd get a phone call one day and hear the same news about her uncle.

Austin reached over and patted her hand. "Don't feel bad. Everything worked out for the best."

She looked down to see his hand on hers, her hand all warm and tingly where their skin touched. *This is **not** a date*, she sternly reminded herself.

"Um, how was work?" she asked, desperate to steer things back to more neutral territory. "Have you decided where to put the tree?"

They were about to pass the gas station from the other night when Austin hit the brakes and swerved into the parking lot. "Sorry about that." He grinned when he saw the startled look on her face. "I forgot about the pizza! Be right back."

He was out of the truck before she had time to process what was going on. She'd forgotten about the pizza as well, and once again, did not have the money to pay for it. A cup of coffee was one thing; a whole meal—even if it was just pizza—was another.

While Austin was inside, she checked the bank app on her phone, then sighed in relief when she saw her last paycheck had been deposited. It wasn't much, since they'd fired her in the middle of a pay period, but she'd at least be able to pay for a few things until she got back on her feet.

"I hope you still like pepperoni," he said as he got back in the truck. He set the box between them, then handed her a bottle. "And I hope you still like root beer." He gave her a sheepish look. "I probably should have asked before I went inside."

"Still love them both," she replied, accepting the bottle he handed her. "Tell me how much I owe you and I'll send it to you."

Austin shrugged. "Don't worry about it. It's the least I can do since you're giving up your free time to help me with this 'much-needed' project," he teased.

Tess rolled her eyes. "Trust me, you'll thank me once you walk into work tomorrow and see how festive the store looks!"

"I still have my doubts, but we'll see." He pulled back onto the road, then navigated his way out of town.

They rode in silence as Tess tried to come up with a topic that was both safe and interesting. "Is there anyone else in town who went on to become famous?" she asked, curious to know if there were other things she'd missed out on over the last few years.

He thought about it for a minute, then shook his head. "Not that I know of. A lot of our classmates left town," he gave her a pointed look, "but none of them made it big as far as I've seen." He took another bite of pizza, chewing thoughtfully, then slapped the steering wheel. "I just remembered—we do have that famous child actor who moved to town. He's the new drama teacher at the high school. In fact, the drama club is putting on a play next week. You should go check it out if you get the chance."

The fact he did not offer to go with her did not go unnoticed, but that shouldn't surprise her. How many times had she claimed she was just here to visit? She'd given him zero reasons to invest in spending time with her. "I'll think about it," she replied, with zero intention of actually going.

"If you do decide to go, let me know," he said as he pulled into the parking lot of the tree farm. "There's a large group of us going on Christmas Eve, and you're welcome to tag along."

His offer felt like an afterthought, but what did she expect? Tess was spared from answering when he pulled into a parking spot and hopped out of the truck. She quickly followed, just as eager to get this over with as he appeared to be.

They wandered from section to section of pre-cut trees, but none of them stood out to her until they found the Fraser Fir trees.

"This one," Tess said, pointing to a gorgeous eight-foot-tall tree.

Austin raised a brow but dutifully grabbed the tree. "Think you can handle carrying the top if I carry the bottom?"

"Sure," Tess replied.

He lowered the top down to her, then picked up his end. It was a struggle, but they managed to make it to the front where the cashier was stationed.

"You know I have, like, zero decorations, right?"

Tess's breath caught in her throat at his announcement. "And you didn't think to tell me that before now?"

"I assumed you knew!" he shot back. "I've told you repeatedly I don't decorate for Christmas. Plus, I own a feed store, so I have no reason to sell ornaments."

"Okay, fine," she said. She took a deep breath and tried to formulate a plan. "We'll just have to stop by Dollar General on the way back." She was now deeply regretting her decision to get such a big tree, but she would find a way to make it work if it was the last thing she did.

***

It took them an hour to get back to the feed store, the trip to Dollar General taking much longer than expected; however, the time was not spent in vain. While Austin drove, Tess searched Pinterest on her phone, and by the time they arrived, she was ready to create the best Christmas tree anyone had ever seen!

"You set the tree up while I grab some things from the shelves," Tess commanded. She grabbed a cart, then began to peruse the aisles of the feed store. When she was done, she went back to the front of the store, delighted to see the tree in place.

"What do you have there?" Austin asked, peering into the cart. He began to pick up items. "Twine, dog biscuits, pet toys?" He quirked his brow. "You're going to decorate with these?"

Tess snatched the adorable mouse toy out of his hand, then shook it at him. "Oh ye of little faith," she teased. "Stand back and prepare to be amazed!"

"As you wish." He went back behind the counter and took a seat, resting his head on his hands.

She was tempted to sarcastically offer him popcorn for the show but managed to hold her tongue. This was supposed to be fun, not an excuse to be combative. "Do you have a ladder?" she asked as she pulled the white lights out of the bag of decorations she purchased.

Austin walked to the back of the store, then returned with a rickety old ladder that looked like it was older than them. "You should let me do this," he told her as he set the ladder up.

"I can handle a ladder," she said, rolling her eyes. She stomped up the side, her irritation on full display. "You men are always so sexist. Women are just as capable of climbing a ladder as—" Tess screamed as the ladder wobbled, causing her to lose her balance, her foot slipping off the rung as she fell backward. She braced for impact, then opened her eyes wide as she landed on something soft instead.

"You were saying?" Austin said as he cradled her in his arms.

His eyes darkened as he stared down at her, and for just a moment, she thought he was going to kiss her. Instead, he put her down on her feet, then let go as soon as she was steady.

"Would it have killed you to hold the ladder for me?" she asked grumpily.

Without a word, he took the lights from her, climbed the ladder, then began to wrap them around the tree. Even though she was now irritated, she did her part by connecting the strands together as he went. It took a while, but they got it done.

"Okay, next up are the ribbons," she announced as she grabbed the red and green plaid from the bag. "Want to have a little race?" she asked, her brow raised in challenge.

Austin grinned. "That depends. What does the winner get?"

"Hmm." Tess tapped her finger against her chin. "Loser has to wear this reindeer headband at the festival Saturday," she said, pulling the headband out of the bag to show him.

He took the headband, placed it on his head, then checked his reflection in the window. "I think this will look good on you," he replied.

"You wish, buddy," she teased. "We both know I'm going to win this competition, so get used to wearing that thing!"

"How confident in that are you?" He removed the headband and placed it on her head. "Confident enough to wager something a little more personal?"

A shiver of excitement raced down her spine. "Like what?"

"Loser has to kiss the winner?"

They were playing a dangerous game, and they both knew it, but Tess wasn't about to back down now. "You're on."

She handed him a ribbon, then went to work making ribbons as fast as she could and tying them to the tree. Before she knew it, she was out of ribbon; however, when she looked over to see where Austin was, he still had half a roll left. "What happened?" she asked, taking the roll from him. She looked at the ribbons he'd placed on the tree and laughed. "Those are gorgeous, but you can't seriously expect to win a race with those," she said as she admired the complex bows he'd created.

"Who said I was trying to win?" He grinned at her, then leaned down and kissed her cheek.

For the second time that night, disappointment washed over her. Was he trolling her? Why make a bet like that and then lose on purpose just to kiss her cheek—unless he was trying to send a message?

"I'll take care of the rest," she said, stepping away from him to grab the red Christmas ornaments.

Without a word, he went and hopped on the counter, presumably to watch her work.

It was hard, but she managed to pretend he wasn't there, choosing instead to focus on the task at hand. When she was done, she stepped back to admire her work. Bows made from plaid ribbon adorned the tree, while dog treats dangled from twine. Mixed in were various types of pet toys, small bird feeders, and a small assortment of red bulbs. It was perfect for the feed store, if she did say so herself.

Now that the tree was done, she looked over at Austin, anxious to see his reaction.

He hopped off the counter and stood beside her. "Wow!" he exclaimed, taking it in. "This is amazing!"

The look on his face was worth every second of torture. "I'm glad you like it," she said softly, mesmerized by the lights twinkling in the reflection of his eyes.

"I don't just like it—I love it!" he said, turning his attention to her. He stared into her eyes, then reached out to her, but she sidestepped him and walked away.

"I should get home," she told him. "I'm sure you're exhausted after such a long day. I know I am."

It was his turn to look disappointed, though why he did she couldn't say. He'd made it more than clear he wasn't interested, which was a good thing since she wasn't either. They were just friends. And this wasn't a date. A fact she would repeat as many times as necessary until she finally got it through her thick skull.

The trip out to the farm was as awkward and uncomfortable as she imagined it would be. The silence between them was deafening, their earlier playfulness long gone, replaced with something much closer to hurt and bitterness. He'd barely had time to stop the truck before she was out the door and ready to run inside.

"Hey," he said before she left. "Some of us are getting together Saturday at the Christmas Festival. Would you like to come?"

Too tired to try to make sense of everything, she simply nodded. She could always back out later. Or ghost him, since that seemed to be a popular thing these days.

"Great! Well, have a good night!"

She nodded again, then slammed the truck door and walked inside. Why was life always so complicated? Just once, she wished things would work out exactly how she wanted them to. Says the woman who claimed she wasn't on a date, but very much wished she was.

Chapter 8

To both of their surprises, Jenny showed up to work that morning. Tess wasn't completely off the hook, but it did spare her back since Jenny decided to host a one-woman gingerbread contest and became obsessed with winning.

Since she had some free time, she decided to go for a walk to stretch her legs. For reasons unknown to her, her feet took her to the feed store—against her will, of course. She made it all the way to the door and was just reaching for the handle when she chickened out and turned to leave. With her luck, Austin would think she was stalking him, and she really didn't want him to think that. Especially after their encounter last night.

"Hey Tess, what's up?" Austin called out as he pulled up in a side-by-side.

Of course. She pasted a smile on her face, then furiously wracked her brain for a plausible excuse for why she was there. "Hey, Austin," she said with a wave. "Bye, Austin," she said before hurrying off when her brain failed her. If she had any luck at all, he would let her go and forget all about this awkward encounter.

Beep Beep Beep

“Please don’t mean what I think that means,” she muttered under her breath. When the side-by-side pulled up beside her, she knew Lady Luck had officially abandoned her.

“Hop in,” he called out. “I’ll give you a ride back to the bakery.”

Since she couldn’t very well ignore him, she did as instructed.

“So what brings you out to my neck of the woods?” he asked, obviously biting back a grin.

“I, uh, just wanted to admire my work again,” she finally spit out. Did that sound believable?

Austin pulled up in front of the bakery, then turned to face her. “Is that so?”

“Um, yes?”

“You know, if you wanted to see me again, you could just say so.”

Tess threw her hands up in the air. “Ugh!” she exclaimed. “I was just out for a walk, okay? That’s all it was—nothing more, nothing less.”

“A walk that just so happened to lead you out of the way to my store?” he asked, an amused expression on his face.

Okay, fine. Two could play this little game. “So what do you think I was doing out there then?”

“Obviously, you can’t get enough of me,” he drawled.

That was closer to the truth than she wanted to admit, so she hopped out of the cart and ran inside the bakery, praying all the way he would go back to the store and leave her alone.

Jingle Jingle

Of course. She rested her elbows on the counter, her back to him.

"I was just teasing you," he said softly.

She spun around, just in time to catch the hurt in his eyes. "I don't know why I went to the store," she admitted. "I really was going for a walk and somehow ended up there. Maybe it's because I did the exact same thing the other day and the route felt familiar, or maybe it's because I had fun with you the last couple of nights and wanted to see you again. Regardless, it was a mistake, and it won't happen again."

He stepped closer and stared down into her eyes. "Why was it a mistake?"

"Because we're supposed to be friends, and friends don't do things like that," she replied breathlessly. Was it hot in there? Because she suddenly felt like it was hot.

"I see," he said, taking a step back. "Well, it's good we established that boundary. Wouldn't want anyone to get the wrong idea."

Tess nodded as the memory of him kissing her cheek reared its ugly head. "It's for the best," she agreed, mentally kicking herself for causing whatever this was.

"I guess I'll see you around then." He turned on his heel and stomped toward the door.

"Saturday at the festival, right?" Tess called after him. When he left without responding, she sank into a nearby chair and laid her head in her arms. What had she done?

"Ahem," Jenny noisily cleared her throat. "Is this a bad time?"

Tess groaned, then lifted her head. Of course there would be a witness to her humiliation. "How long have you been standing there?"

"Long enough," Jenny replied. "But don't worry about it, I won't say anything." She stared at Tess for a moment, then turned away as if embarrassed. "Can you give me a hand when you're ready?"

"Be right there," Tess replied. She took a moment to gather her thoughts, then followed Jenny to the kitchen, for once grateful for the distraction from her problems.

***

The next couple of days flew by at the bakery, but the nights, when everything was calm and still, passed by at a snail's pace. It was now Friday, exactly one week since her life had imploded, and things were just as bleak today as they were then. She'd sent out dozens of job applications, and not one single company had called. Not a single 'friend'—local or back in Chicago—had called either. This was supposed to be the most wonderful time of the year, and all she felt was hopeless and depressed.

"Hey Tess?" Bea called out, waving her arms to get her attention.

Tess looked up from the cupcakes she'd been staring at aimlessly for the last few minutes. "What?" she asked, shaking her head to clear the fog. "Did you need something?"

Bea cocked her head to the side as she studied Tess. "Are you okay? You seem kind of sad."

"I'm fine." Tess pasted on a smile but knew she wasn't fooling anyone—let alone her aunt. "Seriously, I'm okay." She noticed the large box Bea was holding and did her best to contain her groan. *Please don't let that be another delivery,* she thought to herself.

Eventually, Bea held out the box and motioned for Tess to take it. "Can you deliver this for me, please?"

Of course it was another delivery. Tess had spent the last few days delivering goods all over town. Gingerbread cookies to the elementary school, cupcakes to the middle school, Christmas-themed tea cakes to the library—the list went on and on. Oh well. At least it got her out of the bakery for a while. If she had to ice one more doughnut or frost one more cookie, she might just scream!

"Where to?" Tess asked as she accepted the box.

"This goes to the B&B up the street," Bea replied, as if Tess should know where that was. When she saw the confused look on her face, she continued. "Two-story house, has a sign out front that says 'Enchanted Holiday Hideaway.'"

That did not clear things up, but Tess figured she'd just drive around until she found the place. "Be back soon," she called over her shoulder.

What should have been a quick three-minute drive took ten minutes, but Tess eventually found the place. It would have been helpful if Bea had specified which street the house was 'up,' but to be fair, Tess hadn't asked either.

She grabbed the box and made her way to the front door, taking in all the holiday decorations on the way. Whoever ran this B&B had spent a lot of time turning it into a scene reminiscent of a Dickens Christmas. Tess was almost tempted to drive by at night to see it in all its lighted glory.

When she reached the door, she hesitated. Should she ring the doorbell or just walk in? It was technically a business, but it also looked like someone's house. She decided to play it safe and ring the bell.

Ding Dong

The cold began to seep in through her jeans as she waited—not so patiently—for the owner to come to the door. She was just starting to regret her decision to ring the bell when the door swung open, revealing a harried-looking Grace Parker.

"Oh! Hey Tess," she said, stepping back so Tess could enter. She shut the door behind them, then hurried to another room, Tess following close behind. "Can you set those on the counter, please?" she said, nodding toward a counter in the adjoining kitchen area.

Tess did as requested, then turned back to see three baby carriers lined up on the dining room table, Grace frantically checking on each baby. "I had no idea you had kids," Tess said, stunned to see someone she knew had triplets. "To be honest, I'm kind of shocked you haven't dragged Cole down to the courthouse by now."

Grace looked at Tess in horror. "Oh no, these aren't mine," she said quickly. "I'm just babysitting for Molly and two of my guests while they're out skiing for the day."

She laughed, relaxing a bit as she checked on the babies again. "I wouldn't have to drag Cole to the courthouse. If he ever suspected there was even a ghost of a chance I was carrying his child, that man would drag me down there!" She looked fondly at the sleeping babies. "Although, to be fair, I wouldn't put up a fight!"

An awkward silence came over them as Tess tried to figure out how to get out of there without appearing rude.

"It's not easy coming home again, is it?" Grace asked softly.

"Why do you say that?" Tess asked in surprise. Was there a neon-flashing sign above her head announcing to the world how she was feeling? Or was it just that obvious how out of place she was?

"Have a seat," Grace said, pointing to a chair at the end of the table. She walked over to the kitchen, then returned a few minutes later with two steaming mugs of peppermint tea, placing one in front of Tess, then taking a seat across from her. "Change is hard," she said, taking a sip of tea. "A lot has changed since you left—but very little, at the same time. I can only imagine how hard it is to come home to a place that feels familiar yet different."

For the first time since she'd arrived back in Winterwood, Tess felt like someone understood. "It feels like everyone grew up and moved on, and I'm still trapped in high school," Tess reasoned out. "I know it sounds strange, but all of my old friends are now married or in committed relationships. They have their own homes, businesses, lives..."

"Don't you have that too?" Grace asked. "I heard you're only visiting for the holidays."

One of the babies began to fuss, so Grace hurried to pick her up, then began to rock back and forth in her seat.

As Tess watched, she debated telling Grace her shameful secret. She had no idea why she would—they were never friends—yet she felt compelled to tell someone who might understand. Her mind made up, she laid it all out on the table, then sat back and waited for the judgment to come.

Grace's eyes widened as she listened, her shock and horror growing with each new revelation. "I am so sorry," she said once Tess had finished. "I can't even begin to imagine how hard that must have been for you. Thank God you had Bea and Junior!"

Tess studied Grace's face closely, looking for signs she was being sarcastic or insincere, but found none. She really did appear to be genuinely concerned.

"What did you say you did again?" Grace asked, switching the baby from one shoulder to the other.

"I worked for a marketing firm," Tess replied, curious why that mattered.

Grace stood up and walked over to her purse, rummaged around for a minute, then came back and handed Tess a business card. "My friend Molly owns a marketing firm here in town," she told Tess. "She's currently out for the day with my guests, but she should be back in the office Monday. I can't promise she'll be able to help, but if anyone can, it's her."

A ray of hope began to blossom in Tess's chest, but she quickly tamped it down. No need to get excited about what could easily turn into a dead end. Still, the mere possibility was more than what she had when she first arrived. "Thank you so much," she said to Grace. Tears threatened her eyes, so she knew she had to get out of there before she embarrassed herself. "I better get back to the bakery," she said, scooting back her chair. "If you need anything else, please let us know!"

"Will do," Grace said cheerfully. She walked Tess to the door, then gave her a hug. "Don't give up," Grace told her. "It's the season of miracles, and I believe one is heading your way!"

Tess had no idea where this woman got all her positivity, but for once she was happy to roll with it. "Thank you, Grace, I really appreciate it."

"You know where to find me if you ever need a friendly ear!"

The baby began to fuss again, so Grace excused herself, allowing Tess to return to her car before the tears fell in earnest. She sat there for a moment, composing herself as she stared at the business card Grace had given her. Regardless of what came of this, she felt a renewed sense of purpose. Maybe what she'd needed all along was someone to share her burden with. No, that wasn't true—she'd shared all of this with Bea first thing when she'd arrived, and that hadn't helped at all. Oh well, that was a mystery for another day. Time to go back to the bakery for another round of gingerbread cookies. God help her, surviving the holidays would be its own miracle.

Chapter 9

Saturday had arrived and still no word from Austin. Tess had written and deleted too many texts to count, each time losing her nerve right before she hit send. She could only assume this meant their plans for the day were canceled, so she decided to work at the bakery despite Aunt Bea giving her the day off—a decision she instantly regretted the second she flipped the closed sign to open and unlocked the door.

Tess stared in shock at the line that had formed outside. She craned her neck to see how long it was, but it was so far down the street she couldn't tell where their line ended and others began.

"Bet you're glad you came in," Bea said, stepping up beside Tess and handing her a cup of coffee. "You're going to need this," she said, clinking their cups together in a mock toast.

"Was it like this last year?" Tess asked as she took a much-needed gulp of the warm liquid.

Bea nodded. "We stayed busy from the time we opened 'til the time we closed."

That explained the copious amount of cookies she'd iced this week. "Well, might as well get to it," she said, putting on her apron and tying back her hair. "Let the chaos commence!"

The second the door was opened, people flooded the bakery, pushing Bea out of the way in the process. Once she'd made it safely behind the counter, she ordered the customers to form two lines, each of them manning a register. By the time the steady stream had reduced to a trickle, they were out of baked goods and anxious to flip the sign back to closed.

"Whew!" Tess said, wiping her forehead with a cloth. "I don't think I've ever worked this hard in my entire life!"

"It was a challenge," Bea agreed. "I made twice as many goods as last year, and we still didn't have enough! I'm glad this will be someone else's problem next year."

Tess threw her arm around Bea's shoulders. "Aww, come on, you know you're going to miss all this."

"Maybe," Bea replied, though she didn't seem convinced. She grabbed her purse, pulled out a few bills, then handed them to Tess. "I appreciate your help—I couldn't have survived this without you—but it's time for you to go to the park and hang out with your friends."

"If it's okay with you, I'd rather just go home," Tess replied, ignoring the money Bea was trying to give her. "My feet are killing me!"

Bea clucked her tongue. "No, it is not okay with me," she said, shoving the money in Tess's pocket. "You've worked hard all week, and now it's time for you to have some fun." She gave Tess an assessing look. "I'll have Junior pick me up so you can have my car. That should help your poor feet."

"Okay," Tess said, too tired to argue. She accepted the keys, grabbed her coat and purse, then gave her aunt a hug. "I'll see you later." What she really meant was she would see her sooner than later, but she left that part out. She said she'd go to the park—she never said she would stay there.

***

The park was so crowded, Tess had to circle the parking area five times to find a spot. She was just about to give up and go home when someone left, creating a space for her. Rather than feel relieved, she felt disappointed—she really wanted to go home. But she promised she would go, so here she was, keeping that stupid promise.

This time, as she wandered through the crowds, she kept her head down, choosing not to bother searching for familiar faces. What was the point? She'd pretty much alienated everyone she cared to see. Monday she would talk to this Molly person and see if she had any leads. With any luck, she'd be out of here by Christmas, and none of this would matter anyway.

As she wandered around, a thought occurred to her: now that Bea was retiring, did that mean they planned to sell the farm? That was a scary thought, especially since her hope of a quick exit seemed more pipe dream than reality these days. There was a very real possibility she was about to be homeless. What would she do? Where would she go? How many times was she going to have this conversation with herself?

Tess was so engrossed in her inner turmoil, she failed to notice the guy in front of her had abruptly stopped walking; she ran straight into the back of him.

"Oh!" she exclaimed, her hand reaching up to rub her nose. "Sorry about that," she announced to the man's back.

The man turned around to check on her. "Are you okay?" he asked, his brow furrowed in concern.

He looked familiar, but Tess struggled to place him—then it hit her. "You're Jake, right?" she asked cautiously, somewhat worried she was mixing Evie's husband with Cassie's boyfriend.

"It's Conor," the man grinned. "I've never been mistaken for a tall, tattooed guy with muscles the size of tree trunks before," he joked.

"In my defense, it's been a long day," Tess replied, her attempt at sounding light-hearted falling flat. "Well, sorry for running into you. I need to pay better attention to where I'm going."

Conor lifted her chin to survey her nose. "You look okay..." he said, turning her head from side to side. "Tired, but okay."

"In that case, I'll be on my way. It was good to see you again, Conor!"

She'd almost made it past him when he reached out and grabbed her arm.

"The others are over there," he said, pointing toward an area that held craft booths. "You should join us—it'll be fun!"

It was tempting to ask who it would be fun for, but she managed to contain her rudeness for once. "Thanks, but I think I'm going to head out. Like I said, it's been a long day."

He grabbed her hand and pulled her toward the booths. "Nonsense, you have to at least say hello first. If the girls can't talk you into staying after that, well, you have a stronger will than most!"

Tess did not want the others to see her holding Conor's hand, so she gently pulled away but, for reasons unknown, continued to follow him. She supposed it wouldn't hurt to say hi—unless, of course, they shunned her. But if that happened, then she'd know for sure she wasn't welcome and needed to leave.

"Look who I found!" Conor announced once they reached the group.

To Tess's surprise, Austin was among them, deep in conversation with a woman who looked like she was at least four months pregnant. Was this the ex-girlfriend Bea had mentioned? If so, was that his baby? That would explain the kiss on the cheek—but not why he proposed the bet in the first place. That part was still a mystery. This was way too much to handle after the day she had.

"Hey everyone..." Tess said, waving awkwardly. "It's nice to see you all again, but I think I need to go. I just ran into Conor—literally—and I've got a bit of a headache, so, if you'll excuse me..." She knew it was rude, but she left without giving them a chance to say a word. If they didn't hate her before, they surely would now.

She was almost to the parking lot when someone called her name.

"Tess, wait up!" Austin called out.

She ignored him and sped up. If she could just make it to the car, it would all be okay.

Austin came into view, jogging from behind to get in front of her and forcing her to stop walking. "Didn't you hear me call your name?" he asked.

"Yes," she said, brushing past him.

"So you're ignoring me?"

"Also yes," she replied.

She finally reached the car and paused to pull out the keys, mentally kicking herself for not having them ready. She was just putting the key in the door when Austin leaned against it.

He stared down at her in silent challenge. "You are a very confusing woman."

Whether it was her exhaustion, the possibility of him having a baby with another woman, or just circumstances in general, those six simple words broke her. "I confuse myself!" she said, choking on a sob. "Now will you please let me go? I've humiliated myself in front of you enough, don't you think?"

Austin sucked in a breath, then pulled her into his arms. "I didn't mean to make you cry," he said gently, holding her tightly against his chest.

Loud voices—followed by the sound of laughter—grew close, effectively putting an end to her little breakdown.

"I'm sorry," she said, stepping out of his arms. "I honestly don't know what's come over me."

"We should go somewhere and talk," Austin suggested. "Somewhere warm and preferably private."

She wasn't sure that was a good idea, but it sounded better than staying here, so she agreed. "We can go to the bakery," she offered. "I'll make you a decent cup of coffee to make up for the slop we drank the other night."

"If you feel up to driving, I'll follow you over there."

A few minutes alone to gather her thoughts sounded pretty good right about now, so she nodded. Once he was gone—presumably to get his truck—she got in the car and rested her forehead against the steering wheel. What was she doing? Besides making a bigger mess of her already messy life.

Since she already committed to this path, there was nothing to do now but follow it. All she had to do was keep it together a little longer. Surely she could handle that. Right?

Chapter 10

When Tess arrived at the bakery, she pulled around to the back, parking in her aunt's usual spot. She briefly waited for Austin to pull in beside her, then got out and went to open the door. To her immense relief, the building was dark, a sign Bea had left for the day. It had not crossed her mind her aunt could still be there until she was already on her way, and by then, it was too late to change destinations.

Austin walked in the door and looked around, his eyes taking in the equipment. "I've never been back here before," he said, his eyes continuing to roam. "Are you sure your aunt won't mind us being here? We could always go somewhere else."

Tess grabbed coffee grounds from the supply closet, then turned on the fancy espresso machine her aunt kept for employee use. "I'm sure," she called over her shoulder. Knowing her aunt, she would love to hear her bakery was the site of some secret rendezvous. Not that it was, of course; it was just two friends having a conversation.

While the coffee brewed, Tess grabbed a couple of stools and placed them near one of the large baking tables. She then scrounged around for a couple of leftover cookies and set them by the stools. Once that was done, she motioned for Austin to take a seat, then proceeded to pour their coffee into the cute little café cups her aunt saved for special occasions, placing one in front of each of them.

"Okay, I think I'm ready to talk," she announced as she took a seat. "What's up?"

"I'm pretty sure you're the one who's supposed to be talking," Austin drawled. "Starting with why you were crying earlier?"

There went her hope he'd overlook that. She blew on her coffee while she tried to come up with a good reason he might believe. When she couldn't, she decided to go with the truth for once. "Things have been pretty overwhelming since I've been back," Tess said slowly. "When I saw you with that woman..." she hesitated, unsure how to say what she wanted to say without sounding like a jealous psycho.

"You assumed she was my ex?" he guessed.

"Yes, I guess I did."

"I see," he said, taking a sip of coffee. "Well, she's not."

Tess's head shot up, her eyes locking with his. "She's not?"

"Nope," he said, shaking his head. "Her name is Vanessa and she's married to a man named Emilio. You don't know them—they moved here after you left—but Emilio is a financial advisor and he's been helping me out with the business and stuff."

Relief washed over her at the news he wasn't having a baby with another woman.

"A better question is why do you care?" he asked.

He appeared to be genuinely curious, as opposed to angry or rude or whatever you wanted to call it, but she still didn't like that question. Why *did* she care? All she'd talked about since she first arrived was how badly she wanted to leave. So why did it matter who Austin did or didn't date, or whether or not he had a baby with someone? It was none of her business, and yet, she did care. In fact, she hated the thought of him with someone else.

"I don't know," she said, her voice barely above a whisper. Since she couldn't bring herself to face him, she hopped off the stool and grabbed his cup. "It looks like you could use a refill."

She walked over to the machine and busied herself with making another cup. She was so engrossed in what she was doing, she didn't hear him come up behind her. Nor did she see his hands come to rest on the counter on either side of her.

"Aren't you tired of lying to yourself?" Austin whispered against her hair.

Tess was so startled, she jumped, her back coming up against his chest. When he reached over to steady her, he held her in place, her head leaning back against his shoulder.

"Why does this feel so right?" she asked helplessly. She clasped his hands in hers, hugging his arms around her waist.

"Are you happy?" he asked. "In Chicago, I mean. Because if you are, I will march right out of here and never bother you again. I've already promised I won't get in the way of your dreams, Tess. But if you're not happy..."

It took her a moment to process his question; it was too important for her to get the answer wrong. "I thought I was," she finally said. And she had. But how real was that happiness? More importantly, how real were her relationships if it was so easy for the people she thought were her friends to ghost her in her time of need? She wouldn't have done that to them.

"And now?" he prompted.

"Now… I'm not so sure," she admitted. Pain coursed through her as she said those words, but so did relief. She was finally coming to terms with things, and while it hurt to discover her life hadn't been as great as she thought, it also gave her a sense of freedom. Freedom to forge a new future instead of trying to recreate the past.

Austin let go of her and gently turned her around to face him. He then lifted her chin with his finger, so he could look into her eyes.

"I don't know what to do with you," he said, his voice hoarse with emotion. "Part of me wants to kiss you until you finally realize this is where you've always belonged. The other part knows you need time to figure things out on your own."

"Is that why you proposed that stupid bet Tuesday night and then kissed me on the cheek?" she asked bitterly.

His arms tightened around her, preventing her from running away.

"I made that bet because I was dying to kiss you," he admitted. "But while we were making those bows, I realized I was being unfair to you. To us. I'm not interested in a temporary fling, Tess, and I don't think you are either."

She wanted to argue, but she knew he was right; her heart could not handle temporary, not when it came to him. So where did that leave them? She knew what she needed to do, she just really didn't want to do it. It was time to be honest. Completely honest. No more lies, no more half-truths.

But first, she reached up and pulled his face down to hers, her lips meeting his in a slow and sensual kiss. When she felt confident she'd properly conveyed her feelings in a way her words never could, she pulled back, then put some distance between them.

"What was that for?" he asked, his voice tinged with awe.

Tess swallowed hard, then looked into his eyes. "I haven't been honest with you," she informed him, her voice strong and sure. She launched into her tale, sparing no detail—even the ones that made her look sad and pathetic—including how she'd been too embarrassed the other night to tell him she didn't have money for the coffee. By the time she was done, she felt like she'd purged her soul.

Austin ran his hand through his hair, then walked back to the table and sat down. "That was... a lot," he said, blowing out his breath. He sat there for a moment, staring off into space, before turning back to her. "I don't know what to say."

"There's not much to say," she said, joining him at the table. "I know I lied about why I was here, but I was honestly so embarrassed I didn't know what else to do. Part of me hoped I would find another job before the holidays were over and no one would ever be the wiser."

"I guess that makes sense," he said, still not looking at her. "So where does that leave you now?" he asked, his sentiment echoing hers.

The hope in his eyes was hard to bear. It was obvious he wanted her to say she planned to stay, but she couldn't do that. Even if her future wasn't back in Chicago, it wasn't in Winterwood either. A job like hers could only be found in a city, and even if she could find one in a city nearby, that still didn't guarantee they could jump the hurdles that would bring. Unless, Molly was hiring...

"For now, my future is unclear," she replied.

"Then it sounds like nothing has changed," he said sadly. "Unless you think my plan to kiss you until your future becomes clear would work?"

"Is there a third option?" Tess asked hopefully. "One where you pretend I'm not a hot mess and we spend the rest of the night enjoying the festivities together?"

A grin slowly spread across his face. "That sounds like a fair compromise."

That surprised her, but it was a good surprise. To be honest, she'd expected him to be angry, to tell her what a lying jerk she was and that he never wanted to see her again. The fact that he didn't was another Christmas miracle. At this point, she was using up so many miracles, she was beginning to fear there wouldn't be any left for the things she really needed: like a job and a place to live.

When Austin held out his hand, Tess eagerly took it. She knew she wasn't being fair, but right now all she wanted was to forget about her problems and spend time having fun with him. Tomorrow was another day, and with it would come another opportunity to stress.

"Shall we?" he asked. When they stood, he twirled her around, then pulled her back to him.

Tess laughed, her arms automatically clasping around his neck.

This time, it was he who leaned down to kiss her, his lips brushing hers until he left her breathless.

"What was that for?" she asked, mimicking his earlier reaction.

"Just wanted to make sure my intentions are clear," he said, grinning from ear to ear. "Don't want any more misunderstandings like we had last Tuesday."

They walked out of the bakery hand-in-hand, Tess opting to leave Bea's car there and ride with Austin back to the park. If they were quick, they would make it just in time to see the parade and watch the Christmas tree lighting ceremony.

This was truly turning out to be a magical day; Tess just wished she didn't have this sinking feeling in the pit of her stomach.

Chapter 11

Tess paced in front of the bakery window, her anxiety growing by the second. It was finally Monday—the day she was to call Molly—but she was so stressed out, every time she picked up the phone to dial her number, her fingers shook too much to push the correct numbers. *She's just a person*, Tess reminded herself. A person who just might hold her future in her hand.

"Honey?" Bea called, startling Tess when she put her hand on her shoulder. "What on earth has got you so wound up?" She gave Tess an assessing look. "You didn't have another spat with Austin, did you?"

As far as she knew, things with Austin were going okay... well, as much as they could be given the circumstances. She hadn't seen him since Saturday night, but they'd parted on good terms, so that was something. "Do you know a woman named Molly?" Tess blurted out.

Taken aback by the abrupt change in topic, Bea removed her hand and moved to a chair. "Sit down," she commanded, motioning toward the opposite seat. "Of course I know Molly," she said once Tess had sat. "What about her?"

"Grace suggested I contact her today and ask if she knows anyone who's hiring," Tess explained. "Thing is, I don't really know what to say."

"That's a great idea!" Bea exclaimed. "I'm embarrassed I didn't think of it." She tapped her finger against her chin. "What to say about Molly..." she mused out loud. "Well, for starters, she's from Boston, has a take-no-prisoners way about her, and from what I've heard, is very good at her job."

Tess was surprised to hear Molly was from Boston. A woman who traded city life for small-town living, yet she was somehow making it work. Interesting. "Is she nice?" Tess asked. She knew she sounded childish, but some of the people she'd worked with over the years had been cutthroat and proud of it. If Molly was like that, Tess wanted to know in advance so she could prepare herself.

"Nice, but honest," Bea replied. She stood up, ready to go back to work. "Give her a call. Stressing about it accomplishes nothing."

Alone again, Tess pulled out her phone and stared at it. She could do this. Of course, there was the awkwardness of having to introduce herself. What should she say? "Oh, to heck with it," she said, dialing the number.

"Winterwood Brand Boutique, this is Molly speaking."

"Um, hi Molly, this is Tess Wilcox. Grace Parker gave me your number..."

"Hi Tess! I've been expecting your call. Grace says you're a marketing expert?"

Expert was a bit of a stretch. Tess had no idea how Grace had come to that conclusion, but maybe she was trying to help out by boosting Tess's reputation a bit. If that were the case, she appreciated it—but how should she reply to that?

"I have a degree in Marketing, as well as four years' experience," Tess said truthfully. No sense in exaggerating when her résumé would fail to back her up.

There was silence on the other end for a moment, causing Tess's anxiety to amp up again.

"It looks like I have some time around noon. Would that work for you?"

"I'll make it work," Tess blurted out. She smacked her forehead, annoyed at how desperate she sounded. "Thanks, Molly. I'll see you then." She hung up before she made things worse. If she didn't get her act together soon, she would blow this opportunity, and she simply could ***not*** afford that.

Now that she'd completed her task, she returned to the kitchen where Bea was baking cupcakes.

"How'd it go?" Bea asked, looking up from the mixer.

"We have a meeting at noon," Tess informed her. "Would you mind if I went home to clean up and change into something more professional?"

"Of course not, honey. Do whatever you need."

Tess nodded as she turned to leave, only to pause at the odd tone in Bea's voice. "Why do I get the feeling we haven't seen the end of the baking rush?"

Bea grinned. "Because we still have a ton of pies, cupcakes, cakes, cookies, and pastries to bake," she replied. "The Festival is over, school is out for the holidays, but people still have parties to host—not to mention Christmas is only days away!"

"Okayyy," Tess said, taking a deep breath to calm her nerves. "I'll be back as soon as my meeting with Molly is over to help you tackle the list."

It was going to be a long week, and by the time it was over, she had a feeling she would never want to bake again.

***

Tess checked her reflection in the mirror. She was wearing her best pantsuit, black heels, and a pair of glasses that made her look smart but were actually clear glass instead of prescription lenses. Her brown hair was tied back in a simple knot at her nape, her makeup minimal yet effective. Simply put, she looked professional, but she'd never felt like more of a fraud.

What happened to her? One week back in her hometown and suddenly her whole identity was gone. Was it possible to be both a chic marketing executive who wears power suits *and* a small-town girl who wears flannel and bakes cookies? She supposed she was about to find out.

Embarrassed by her vanity, she ditched the glasses, left her empty leather briefcase in the closet, and shook her hair out, allowing it to fall in loose waves down her back. She looked in the mirror again, this time smiling at the woman looking back.

"I can do this!" she announced to her reflection. Now satisfied with her appearance, she grabbed her phone and purse, then headed to the car, waving to Junior as she passed by.

Ten minutes later, she parked in front of the address listed on the business card, then did a double take as she realized where she was. Molly must be doing really well if she was able to afford this building. Back in the day, it had been a manufacturing building or something like that. All Tess knew was the building was HUGE!

Her hand shook as she opened the door—whether from the cold or nerves was anyone's guess—but she held her head high as she walked in, determined to exude confidence even if that was the last thing she felt.

"Can I help you?" a tall man with dark wavy hair asked.

Tess wasn't an expert, but she was certain the man's suit cost more than a month's salary. What was going on here?

He quirked a brow, then cleared his throat.

"She's here to see me," a voice called out.

The man smiled, then nodded. "Ah, you must be Tess," he said, holding out his hand. "I'm Grant, Molly's husband. Nice to meet you."

Tess gave herself a mental shake, then shook his hand. "Sorry about that," she said, smiling self-consciously. "I'm a little nervous."

Grant pointed to a door at the end of the hall. "She's in there," he said. "I swear she doesn't bite!" he joked, his voice low enough only she could hear.

That was the encouragement Tess needed to get moving. She marched into Molly's office, her hand automatically extending as she introduced herself.

"It's so nice to meet you," Tess said warmly. "I've heard a lot about you!"

"That would explain your nerves," Molly joked. "Please, have a seat," she said, indicating one of the chairs opposite her desk. "Grace said you lost your job. Care to tell me what happened?"

Bea hadn't been kidding when she said Molly was honest—no beating around the bush with her, that was for sure. Tess took a breath, then squared her shoulders. "I got laid off due to downsizing," she stated matter-of-factly. "You know the drill—company reports record profits for the year, then lays off half their staff."

Molly nodded sympathetically. "I've been there myself a time or two," she replied. "Do you have a résumé for me?"

Tess froze at what should have been a logical expectation. "Is it okay if I email you a copy?" she asked, her face scrunched in embarrassment. "I'm staying with my aunt and uncle, and they aren't the most tech-savvy..." When Molly nodded, Tess pulled out her phone and sent the email, double and triple checking the résumé was attached before she hit send. The last thing she needed was to look incompetent in front of Molly.

"All right, let's see what we've got here," Molly said, her eyes glued to her computer screen. "This seems to match what you told me on the phone. What made you decide to go into marketing?"

How does one answer a question like that? She'd never known a single person who said they wanted to be a marketer when they grew up, including her. Most people tend to focus on the selling aspect, but that has never been her thing. That might have been why she was one of the ones laid off, now that she thought about it. "I've always liked telling stories in a way that resonates with people," she replied honestly. "To me, it's about the experience. I like to create campaigns and build brands around connection. Specifically, helping brands form relationships with their customers."

"That's a good answer," Molly said, nodding along. "I have a couple of contacts I can reach out to who are currently hiring," she informed her. "I take it relocating is not an issue?"

To her surprise, her heart seized a bit at the mention of leaving, which was ridiculous since she'd known all along that would be the outcome. Not to mention she'd claimed for the better part of a decade she wanted to live anywhere but here. So why was she suddenly reluctant to leave? Was it because she was scared to go through the process of moving and starting a new job, only to end up back here again? Or perhaps because she'd reconnected with her family and was reluctant to leave again? No—while both of those were true, the reason was Austin. She'd been right to avoid a relationship with him all those years ago, and if she'd been smart, she would have done the same thing this time too. But no, she just had to go and get her feelings all tangled up in a dream that would never become reality, and now two people would be hurt by her reckless decisions.

"Okay, looks like that *is* an issue," Molly said after a long pause.

Tess shook her head. "No, I'm prepared to do whatever I have to do to secure a job."

"Hmm." It was clear Molly did not believe her. "Give me a couple of days to see what I come up with."

"Thank you," Tess replied. She stood, then proffered her hand a second time. "I really appreciate this. I know it's a lot to ask of a stranger."

"You're not really a stranger," Molly said with a laugh. "Several of my friends have known you for years, and in a town like Winterwood, that practically makes you family!"

A wave of sadness washed over Tess. She'd treated this town—and everyone in it—with disdain for most of her life, yet here they were, welcoming her with open arms. The problem had never been the town, its people, or even its lack of opportunities. The problem had always been her, and now that she finally realized it, she would have to leave again.

"Thank you again." Tess did her best to smile, then left as fast as her three-inch heels would carry her. As she passed through the lobby, she took in all the decorations she'd been too nervous to see when she'd first arrived. Someone had spent a lot of time on them. Why that bothered her, she couldn't say. She walked back to Molly's office. "Can I ask why you left Boston to move here? It couldn't have been easy to start a marketing agency in the middle of nowhere."

Molly looked up from the computer screen, a thoughtful expression on her face. "I would like to say it's because I wanted a simpler way of life," she said slowly. "In fact, I'm pretty sure that's the excuse I gave my boss when I handed in my two weeks' notice. My husband and I worked so much, we practically became strangers, and to be honest, I really wanted kids and the whole nine yards, ya know?"

Tess nodded. She wanted those things too.

"But if I'm being honest, Grant and I work almost as much here as we did there." She gave a wry smile. "What we were really missing was the community—not that you can't have that in a big city," she added quickly. "It's just, there's something special about this town. I knew it the moment I arrived and witnessed with my own two eyes the entire town come together for my friend in her time of need. That's when I decided I wanted to stay."

"I appreciate your honesty," Tess said sincerely. "I'll let you get back to work."

Tears spilled down her cheeks as she walked back to the car. She should be thrilled right now. Molly had promised to talk to her contacts, and Tess had zero doubts she would have some leads by the time they spoke next. Instead, all she felt was a sense of despair. She really was a hot mess.

Chapter 12

Tess was too wound up to go back to the bakery, so she drove to the feed store instead. When she pulled into the lot, Austin was coming around the side of the building. As soon as he recognized her, he hopped into the passenger seat.

"Wow, you look... like you belong in a boardroom somewhere," he said as he looked her up and down, taking in her pantsuit and heels. He took a deep breath, then turned to face forward. "Is that why you're here? To tell me you're leaving?"

She reached over and took his hand in hers, lacing her fingers through his. "No, I'm not leaving," she sighed. "Not yet, anyway."

"Then what's with the outfit?"

"I met with a woman who may have connections that will lead to a job," she explained. "But—"

He squeezed her hand. "But if you get a job, you'll be leaving," he finished for her.

They sat in silence for a moment, each clinging to the other as they processed what this meant for their relationship.

"You could stay and work at the bakery," Austin proposed. "I'm sure Bea would love the help!"

"She's retiring and selling the bakery to someone else," Tess informed him. "While it's possible I could work for the new owner, I really don't want to work at the bakery," she moaned. She leaned her head against his shoulder, snuggling as close as she could in the small space.

Austin chuckled, then leaned his head against hers. "You could always work at the feed store with me!"

It was likely he was kidding, but the idea held some appeal. She could imagine sneaking kisses when the customers weren't looking, like they were teenagers again.

"I suppose there's no chance you would ever come with me, is there?" she asked, even though she already knew the answer.

He sighed and looked out the passenger window. "Why don't we see what happens before we make any life-altering decisions, okay?" He turned back to her, then kissed the top of her head. "I need to get back to work. Want to have dinner tonight?"

Tess's head snapped up in surprise. She'd expected him to distance himself while they waited to see what happened with Molly, but was thrilled to see he wasn't doing that. Though she hated to admit, it would be easier on both of them if he did. "I would love to," she replied, throwing caution to the wind. "What do you have in mind?"

"How about you come over to my place and I'll throw some steaks on the grill?"

"In this weather?" Tess asked, her gaze drifting toward the snow-covered ground.

Austin shrugged. "It's not ideal, but grilled meat is my specialty! I've got to impress my date, you know!"

"Okay then," she replied. Who was she to stand between a man and his grill? "I'll bring dessert. Just text me your address when you get a minute so I know where to go."

"Same place you've been a thousand times." He opened the door and stepped out, then waved goodbye before closing the door behind him.

She watched him walk inside, completely dumbfounded to learn he still lived with his parents. Was she the only one who thought bringing a date over for dinner when your parents were in the next room was weird? Oh well, she doubted this was the first time he brought a woman home, so she would just have to roll with it.

The clock on the dashboard claimed it was a little after one, which meant she had plenty of time to change her clothes and get back to the bakery. At least today was pie day. That was a nice change from all the cookies she baked.

***

It was six o'clock on the dot when Tess pulled up to the old farmhouse. The sun had set, but the moon was full, bathing the area in a soft, warm glow. She could easily take a picture and claim it was one of those postcards from the fifties—well, if she removed Austin's truck.

She grabbed the bakery boxes and approached the door, surprised to see it open before she had a chance to knock. "You must be eager to see me," she teased.

Austin grinned at her, then moved back so she could enter. "You were always punctual to a fault when we were kids," he reminded her. "I just assumed that hadn't changed."

"I suppose that's fair," she agreed. She handed him one of the boxes. "I also made an assumption that pecan pie is still your favorite." She then held up the other box. "And these are cookies for your parents!"

A pained look crossed his face, turning his grin into a frown.

"What's wrong?" Tess asked, immediately concerned she'd put her foot in her mouth again. "If you don't think they'll like the cookies, I can always run back to the bakery and grab something else."

"My parents passed away six years ago," he said quietly. "My dad had a heart attack one day while he was out in the field. By the time we found him, it was too late." He took a deep breath and turned away. "My mom passed a month later due to complications from pneumonia."

Tess gasped, her hand covering her mouth as she stared at him in horror. "I am so sorry," she said, her words coming out in a rush. "Why didn't you tell me? We had that whole conversation about Lyle Sr. and his stroke the other night..." She shook her head, absolutely floored by his news.

"Honestly, I thought you knew," he said, no longer meeting her gaze.

He thought she knew but never said anything to him? Just like he thought she knew he purchased the feed store and never said anything. "Why are you still friends with me?" she asked, completely flabbergasted by what she was hearing. "Like, how can you possibly stand to even be in the same room as me if you think I am so cruel and heartless that I would let you suffer from such a huge loss alone?"

"You were busy at school," he mumbled, clearly uncomfortable. "I better check the grill—don't want the steaks to burn..."

She was so hurt that she was tempted to leave, but then she thought about Austin and how he must have felt all these years. It's not like he was wrong to assume she knew; this was clearly something her aunt would have mentioned. So why didn't she? Had Tess been so caught up in her own life this was one more thing she'd ignored? She tried to come up with other possible scenarios but couldn't. Wow, she wasn't just a jerk, she was a selfish jerk. Why anyone was willing to give her a second chance was beyond her comprehension—she clearly didn't deserve it.

Now she was left to wonder if she should leave to spare him any further pain, but that felt like taking the coward's way out. So she did the only thing she could and followed him out to the deck. She made her way to the back of the house, then walked outside and put her arms around his waist, leaning her forehead against his back. "I'm sorry," she said, tightening her arms.

"For what?" he asked, his eyes glued to the grill. His posture was stiff, and he refused to touch her, but he remained where he was.

"For everything," she replied as she bit back her tears. If he knew she was crying, he would comfort her—and for once, it was her turn to do the comforting. "I was a terrible friend in high school who only cared about myself. I was a terrible friend in college, who didn't even bother to call when you lost your parents—though I swear I don't remember hearing that news—and I've been a terrible person since I came back." A small sob escaped, and she coughed to cover it up. "You deserve so much better than me, but I'm so glad you've given me a second chance." This time, when she sobbed, she wasn't able to hide it. "Which makes me even more terrible since I know I'm going to leave soon, and I feel like I'm leading you on, even though I'm not trying to, and all I want is to be with you, but I can't, and—"

Austin turned around and pulled her up against him, his lips crashing down on hers as he kissed her until they were both breathless. He lifted his head, then leaned his forehead against hers. "I accept your apology," he said once he was able to speak.

"Thank you, but we can't keep doing this," Tess whispered. "We agreed we didn't want a temporary fling and—"

He kissed her again, cutting her off.

When they pulled apart, she stared up at him, her eyes narrowed. "You can't keep silencing me like that, mister. You know what I'm saying is true."

"You kissed me first," he reminded her. "All bets were off after that. Now if you'll excuse me, I need to get these steaks off the grill before they burn."

She stepped out of the way, but crossed her arms and continued to glare at him. "Technically you kissed me first, it just so happened to be on my cheek." she snarked. "Anyway, you agree that I've been leading you on, yet you're still hanging out with me? That doesn't make any sense."

"I never agreed to that," he said as he piled meat on a plate. "I simply said you kissed me first. I'm a grown man, Tess. I know what I'm risking here, but I've decided it's worth it." He turned to face her. "You're worth it."

For all her talk of fairness and apologies, she found she couldn't argue with him, even though she knew she should. The truth was, she didn't want to argue—she wanted to believe he was right, even though she knew better.

"The steak smells good," she said rather lamely.

Austin grinned at her. "Wait until you taste it." He led her inside and placed the plate on the middle of the table. "Give me one more minute and we should be ready to eat."

"Anything I can do to help?"

"Nope, I've got things under control." He walked into the kitchen and began to grab items from the fridge, then did a double take when he saw smoke rising from the oven. "That's not good," he said, dropping the containers on the counter and rushing to open the oven door.

Tess watched as flames shot out, then hurried over to help. "Turn off the oven and shut the door!" she ordered.

As Austin did as instructed, Tess rummaged through the cabinets for a box of baking soda. "Let's give it a few minutes, and if the fire doesn't go out by itself, we'll douse it with this," she said, holding up the box.

"Not your first oven fire, I take it?" he asked dryly.

"I learned a lot at the bakery," she said with a shrug.

They stood there for a minute, watching the oven intently as they waited to see what the fire would do. When they were convinced it was safe, they opened the door to find a charred mess.

"So much for impressing you with my cooking skills."

Tess bumped his shoulder with hers. "I'm very impressed, silly. We still have the steak, so all hope is not lost!"

"That's all we have, I'm afraid," he said sadly. "Both the cheesy bread and potatoes were in there," he said, pointing to the oven.

"Don't forget the pie!"

"Steak and pie," he lamented. "If we don't get it together soon, our future children might starve!"

A small gasp escaped at the mention of children as her head snapped toward him. She was ready to read him the riot act, but was instantly mesmerized by the twinkle in his eyes. Her heart melted at the sight of his crooked smile. "You're intentionally trying to get a rise out of me, aren't you?"

His arm wrapped around her waist as he pulled her close. "Maybe," he said, dropping a kiss on her nose. "Or maybe I'm just that confident in our future together."

She should push him away right now and put an end to this madness. Someone was going to get hurt—two someones—if she didn't do something soon. But when she raised her hands to his chest, instead of pushing him away, she pulled him closer, her arms continuing to his neck as she leaned up to kiss him. God help them, when it was time to leave, she wasn't sure she'd be able to do it.

Chapter 13

Tess stomped into the kitchen, her slippers slapping against the linoleum as she made her way to the coffee pot. She pulled a mug out of the cupboard, then slammed the door before filling the cup with the precious elixir. Since it was still too hot to drink, she rummaged through the bottom cupboards for a pan to make eggs, decided she wasn't hungry after all, then shoved the pan back in and slammed that door too.

"Goodness, what did the cupboards do to you?" Bea asked in disbelief.

Surprised to hear her aunt's voice, Tess whirled around to see her sitting at the table. "How long have you been there?" she asked, her eyes narrowed in suspicion.

"Since before you came in here all riled up like a cat in a storm," she said dryly. "Seriously, Tess, what has gotten into you? Did you and Austin have another fight?"

"Why do you always assume every time I'm upset it's because Austin and I fought? It's like you've completely forgotten I have all these other problems I'm dealing with." She plopped into a chair opposite Bea and rested her head on her folded arms.

Bea moved to the chair next to Tess and put her arm around her. "You're right, I'm sorry," she said gently. "It's just, you've spent every night with Austin this week and always seemed so happy when you came home. It seemed like a foregone conclusion that if you're upset, it must have something to do with him."

That made sense, and she wasn't completely wrong. Some of Tess's anger did stem from Austin, but not because they fought. "Today is Friday," Tess mumbled.

"Yes," Bea agreed. "What's so special about Friday?"

Tess lifted her head and sighed. "I'm supposed to follow up with Molly today."

"I see," Bea replied. She grabbed her coffee and took a sip, then reached for the plate of muffins in the middle of the table and pushed them toward Tess. "I take it we're no longer as eager to get out of town as we once were?"

"It doesn't matter, does it?" Tess said bitterly. "Unless I plan to spend the rest of my life working at the gas station, I don't really have a choice. Not that there's anything wrong with that, but I have student loans to pay..." She picked up a muffin and absentmindedly tore it into little pieces. Speaking of student loans, if she didn't earn a paycheck soon, she would become a statistic in more ways than one.

Bea gave her a squeeze. "Things will work out for the best, they always do."

More meaningless platitudes. Was that truly all we humans have to offer in ways of comfort? Sure, it sounded better than 'suck it up buttercup,' but was filling people with false hope truly better? She didn't think so, but then again, what did she know?

"How much time do you think you'll need to meet with Molly today?" Bea asked. "There's only three more days till Christmas, and since we're closed Sunday, today and tomorrow will be brutal."

Tess's eyes widened. Has it really been two weeks since she left Chicago? And now there were only three days till Christmas, and she hadn't shopped for a single present. Nor did she even have money to shop. Ugh! She dropped her head back onto her arms.

"Oh come on," Bea said cheerily. "It won't be *that* bad!"

Easy for her to say; things were going great for her. "Give me a few minutes to get dressed, and I'll be ready to go." She sighed dramatically, then dragged herself off to her room. Why anyone wanted to become an adult was beyond her, all she wanted for Christmas was to go back to her childhood!

***

Bea had been wrong—it absolutely was *that* bad. Not only were they already inundated with more orders than they could possibly fill, a steady stream of customers filed in all morning begging for last-minute goods. And when they were forced to turn them away, more than a few had choice words for them. Like it was their fault the customer waited till the last minute.

By the time Tess checked her watch, hours had passed, yet they'd barely made a dent in the to-do list.

"You should check in with Molly," Bea suggested. "I feel like we're at a good stopping point."

"I'll just give her a quick call and get it over with," Tess replied. "Then I'll get back to work."

"Sounds good," Bea agreed. "Feel free to use my office so you can have some privacy."

It took a few minutes for Tess to work up the courage to make the call. Worse than moving to Timbuktu was the possibility Molly had reached out to her contacts and come up empty-handed. Since Tess still hadn't heard anything from any of the other places she applied to, this was a real concern. Either companies really weren't hiring right now, or they didn't want to hire her.

Ring Ring

Startled, Tess dropped the phone on the table, then quickly picked it up to see Molly's name on the screen. "Hi Molly, I was just about to call you!"

"Hey Tess, is there any way you can come over to the office real quick? I have some things to discuss with you."

She looked down at her stained shirt and jeans. "Um, yes, but I'll be coming from the bakery so I look, well... less than professional."

"Don't worry about that," Molly replied. "I'll see you in a few."

Tess ended the call, then stared at her phone. Was this a good sign or a bad sign? It seemed unlikely Molly would ask her to come in if she hadn't had any luck; however, she could be the kind of woman who liked to give bad news in person. There was only one way to find out, so Tess grabbed her coat, Bea's car keys, and headed out, waving to Bea as she passed.

When Tess entered Molly's office, she found her sitting at her desk with a baby in her arms.

"I hope you don't mind," Molly said, indicating the baby. "She's fussy today and wants her mama. Don't you!" Molly said, cuddling the little girl.

"I don't mind at all," Tess said, though she was a bit surprised to see a baby in a professional setting. She supposed that was one of the perks of owning your own business.

Molly smiled, then shifted the baby to her shoulder. "So, I have some news," she began, "but I'm not sure you're going to like it."

That was definitely not a good sign. Tess took a deep breath and braced herself for the worst—whatever that was at this point. "I'm ready to hear it."

"I have two possible job opportunities for you," Molly informed her. "Here's the part you might not like. One is in Dallas, Texas, the other is in Tampa, Florida."

"Texas or Florida," she mumbled. Both of those were even farther away than Chicago, and that had already felt like it was in a whole different country. How could she possibly move so far away?

Every fiber of her being wanted to protest, but beggars can't be choosers. "What do I need to do next?" she asked instead.

"If you're sure this is what you want, I'll set up a time for you to meet with your prospective employers, and then we'll go from there."

"That sounds great," Tess replied with the enthusiasm of someone about to receive a root canal. She gave herself a mental shake, then did her best to smile. "Thank you Molly, I really appreciate this."

Molly nodded, her brow knitted in concern. "I'll be in touch as soon as I have a date and time," she replied. "Since it's Friday—and Christmas is Monday—it will probably be some time next week, if not the week after."

Tess had expected that. After all, hadn't she been saying all along that no one hired this time of year? "I look forward to hearing from you." She grabbed her purse and stood. "Merry Christmas."

"Same to you," Molly said, hugging the baby who appeared to have fallen asleep.

Back outside, Tess wrapped her coat tightly around her and power-walked to the car. She should be thrilled right now. After all, this was exactly what she said she wanted, wasn't it?

She took her time driving back to the bakery, which was not an easy feat given how short the distance between them was. When she finally felt ready to return to work, she pulled into the spot in the rear of the bakery, then went back inside.

"So?" Bea asked when Tess entered the kitchen. "What did Molly have to say?"

"Um, she said she has a couple of opportunities in Texas and Florida," Tess told her.

Bea smiled warmly. "Why, honey, that's great news! If you get the job in Florida, I'm sure you can stay with your parents until you get back on your feet. See, things are working out, just like I said they would!"

Bile rose in the back of her throat. "I am NOT moving back in with my parents!" she said vehemently. "Besides that, Florida is a large state. There's no reason to assume my new job will be anywhere remotely close to where they live."

"Honey, I really think it's time to bury the hatchet with your folks. All this anger and bitterness is bad for your soul."

"I don't understand how you have failed to notice they haven't contacted me ONCE since they left," Tess reminded her. "Not one single time! As far as I'm concerned, the hatchet was already buried **in my back** when they decided to leave me behind and move on with their lives as a child-free couple."

Bea appeared taken aback by her anger. "I don't think it's that simple," she said gently.

"Not that simple?" Tess asked incredulously. "If what I'm saying is wrong, then where have they been all these years? May I remind you they never came back for a single holiday, birthday, or graduation! I've received no gifts, no cards, no phone calls or texts. In fact, the only reason I know they're still alive is because you keep bringing them up! Although, since it seems you forgot to tell me Austin's parents died, even that might not be true."

"I didn't forget to tell you about Austin's parents," Bea replied. "I chose not to." When Tess raised a brow, Bea shrugged. "You were in college at the time, but that's not the reason. Austin was dating a nice girl and I didn't want to ruin things for them by bringing you back to town when he was in a vulnerable state."

Tess could not believe what she was hearing. "Are you saying you deliberately chose not to tell me about his parents because you thought I would take advantage of him?"

Bea's mouth opened and closed a few times. "Of course not." She reached her hand out toward Tess, then dropped it in defeat. "It's just, we all knew you had no intention of staying in Winterwood. I didn't want you to come back, get close to Austin in his time of need, then hurt him again by leaving. I thought it was better for both of you if you were allowed to follow your paths without causing each other pain."

A part of her could understand where her aunt was coming from—hadn't she berated herself over that very thing recently? The other part was devastated to learn her own family thought she was so callous and cruel she would intentionally hurt someone she cared about. The worst part of all of this is she strongly suspected her aunt was right, and she would have done that very thing—though not intentionally.

"As for your parents, I don't have an answer for their behavior. I just know it isn't doing you any good to hold onto this resentment," Bea said firmly.

"And just how am I supposed to forgive people who've never asked for it?"

"Forgiveness isn't for the other person," Bea told her. "It's for you. You don't need their apologies or excuses, you just need to make the decision to let go of the past and stop letting it influence your future."

Now Tess was really confused. "What does that have to do with anything?" she asked in frustration. She threw her hands up in the air, then clasped them behind her head. "How am I letting my non-existent relationship with my parents influence my future?"

Bea gave her a compassionate look. "Every choice you've made—from the moment they left until now—has been influenced by them," she said softly. "This need you have to prove you're worthy, your inability to let people get close to you because you're afraid that if they do, they'll leave you too. You're enough, Teresa Joy, just as you are. Don't you think it's time to accept that?"

The urge to run out of there and never come back was so strong, Tess had to grip the counter to keep herself in place. It wasn't because Bea was wrong—it was because she was right. Tess's lack of support from her 'friends' was more than enough proof, and even if it wasn't, there was plenty more where that came from.

"Even if you're right," Tess began, still unable to admit it out loud, "how does that help me now?"

Bea came around the counter and pulled Tess into a hug. "Stop making decisions based on what you think you *should* do, and start following your heart."

"That sounds like following the path to ruin," Tess said dryly. "Isn't going where the job is the *adult* thing to do? I can't just stay here and be unemployed because that's what my *heart* wants."

"There are always options, Tess," she replied cryptically. "You just have to look for them."

Was she right? Were things really that simple? Tess didn't think so—but would it hurt to try? An idea popped into her head, one so crazy there was a ninety-nine percent chance it would fail. But if it did, at least she could say she tried. And hey, there was always that one percent chance of success. This was the season of miracles, after all.

Chapter 14

Now that she'd settled on a plan, Tess was determined to follow through with it before she lost her nerve. So, for the second time that day, she took off her apron and headed to Molly's office. Given how crazy her idea was, she probably should have changed into something professional, but it was too late now. If her aunt was right—and things really did work out the way they're supposed to—then how she was dressed wouldn't matter anyway.

When she reached the office, she parked out front, then took a moment to center herself. She'd never been this bold before—at least, not with a potential employer—her shaky hands and nervous smile clear evidence of that. *Molly is still just a person,* she reminded herself. And honestly, what did she have to lose? If she looked at things that way, it became much easier to open the door and actually get out of the car.

Once inside the building, Tess's newfound confidence began to waver when she was greeted with dead silence. Where was everyone? Had they already left for the day? It *was* the Friday before Christmas. If they had, why was the front door unlocked? She was just about to leave when the sound of Christmas music caught her attention.

"Oh no," she muttered to herself. "They're probably having their company Christmas party."

Visions of previous Christmas parties at her old job filled her head: cheap off-brand soda, pizza from one of those chains that offer $2.99 buffets, and Little Debbie Cakes for dessert. If she were honest, she hadn't thought much of it at the time—she'd simply shrugged and enjoyed her time off from work with her friends. Now she recognized how cheap it was for a company who claimed to make millions to put so little thought, effort, and money into rewarding their employees. Maybe inviting herself to the party—and getting a good look at how Molly treats her employees—would be a good way to see if she actually did want to work here. That decided, she squared her shoulders, then marched toward the music.

Before she entered, she paused, pulled out her phone, then emailed Molly her portfolio. She should have done that the other day when they'd first met, but she'd been too nervous to think about it. When that was done, she reached out and grabbed the doorknob, ready to burst in, then stopped to debate if she should knock first.

"Nah," she shook her head. "Only a weirdo knocks at a company Christmas party." She reached for the doorknob again. "Or talks to themselves out loud where people can hear..."

The door opened, Tess jerking forward along with it.

"Oh!" a man exclaimed. "I'm so sorry, I didn't know anyone was out here."

Of course. Leave it to her to screw up her dramatic entrance. If her life were a movie, it would be a parody.

"What's going on?" Molly asked, coming up beside the man. The baby was still in her arms, but this time she was sound asleep despite all the noise.

"Oh, hi Tess," Molly said when she saw her, her face scrunched in confusion. "Did we have a meeting I forgot about?"

Tess took a quick survey of the room. The only ones there were Molly, Grant, a woman she'd never seen before, the man who opened the door, and Vanessa, the pregnant woman she'd mistook as Austin's ex. That meant either the business was much smaller than she thought, or Molly only hosted parties for the executive-level employees. That thought turned her stomach a little, but it did explain all the name-brand food and drinks she saw.

"Um, no," Tess replied, her cheeks reddening in embarrassment. "I wanted to talk to you, but I can see this is a bad time, so I'll just show myself out."

"Nonsense!" Molly called out as Tess turned to leave. "Come on in and join the party! We can talk while the rest of the guys and gals set up for a riveting game of Trivial Pursuit!"

It did not seem possible to decline a second time without appearing rude, so Tess reluctantly walked into the conference room.

"Where's everyone else?" she asked, unable to hide her distaste any longer.

Molly gave her a strange look. "What do you mean? Who else were you expecting?"

"The rest of your employees!" Tess replied as if it should be obvious. The anger and bitterness that had been festering for the last two weeks bubbled to the surface. "It's always the same with you companies," she said, her head shaking in disgust. "The corporate big-wigs reap all the benefits and rewards while the little guys—you know, the ones that actually do all the work and make all the money—get nothing."

Someone turned off the music, but she was too busy ranting to notice.

"I mean, seriously, you didn't even invite them to the company Christmas party! Or are they somewhere else in the building eating cheap pizza and drinking cheap soda while you guys are in here living it up with all your fancy food and drinks?" Tess's eyes were wide as she looked from one to the other, each of them staring back at her like she'd suddenly grown two heads.

Grant cleared his throat. "I think we should give you two the room," he offered as he motioned to the others to follow him.

"No, you should stay," Molly said, stopping him in his tracks. "You'll want to know what happened anyway—might as well spare me the hassle of having to repeat it." She turned to Tess, her eyes flashing. "I understand losing your job—right before the holidays, to boot—can be traumatic, but that does not give you the right to come in here and throw around baseless accusations. You claim to be a marketing expert, yet had you done a single ounce of research, you would have known that *my* business only has one employee: *me!*"

"But that's not possible," Tess protested. "If you're the only employee here, why are the rest of these people here?" She could feel sweat break out on her back. If what Molly said was true, she'd literally just thrown her entire career down the drain, and for what? A moment of self-righteous indignation?

"Grant and Emilio run a finance company," Molly explained. "That woman over there," she said, pointing to Vanessa, "is Emilio's wife. And that one," she pointed to the other woman, "is their secretary, Celeste. Our companies share the office space, in case that isn't obvious."

Tess blinked back tears. She'd really stepped in it this time, and there was no way she could come back from this.

"I'm really sorry," she choked out. "I—I am so out of line, I just, I have no idea what to say."

The baby began to fuss, and Vanessa stepped forward to take her.

"Thank you," Molly said as she handed her over. She turned back to Tess. "Why don't you tell me why you're here?"

That was the absolute last thing Tess wanted to do. Would it make things worse if she ran out of there instead? It might not make them worse, but it wouldn't make them better. However, that ship had long since sailed so... no, she would not take the coward's way out, no matter how badly she wanted to.

"I came to ask you for a job," she said sheepishly.

Molly narrowed her eyes. "But we already discussed this earlier, remember? I'm supposed to call you within the next few weeks to set up interviews with those companies I told you about."

Tess took a deep breath. "I meant that I came to ask you personally for a job," Tess explained. She looked down at the floor, too embarrassed to look Molly in the eye. "The thing is, while I appreciate you reaching out to your contacts for me, I really don't want to leave Winterwood. I was hoping to convince you I would be a valuable addition to your company. I even emailed you my portfolio," she said with a wry laugh. "Anyway, I'm pretty sure I just torched any chance I may have had with that, so I think it's best I let you guys get back to your party."

This time, when Tess turned to leave, no one stopped her. She made it all the way to her car before the dam broke, tears cascading down her cheeks in rivulets as she rested her forehead against the steering wheel. Why did she keep doing things like this? If she had just waited to hear Molly's explanation after she asked about the other employees, none of this would have happened. Furthermore, if she had done her homework, she would have never asked the question in the first place. Worse than that, it's not like the research would have been hard—she could have literally asked her aunt and within minutes known everything there was to know about Molly, Grant, and their respective businesses.

Ring Ring

She pulled her phone out of her purse and checked the caller ID, for one foolish moment hopeful it was Molly calling to ask her to return. Instead, a name she thought she'd never see again flashed across the screen: Patrick.

"What do you want?" she asked, not even bothering to hide the fact she'd been crying. Who cares what he thought—she owed him nothing.

"Hello to you too," he said, his laugh lighthearted and carefree. *"I expected some hostility, but dang, not that much!"*

Of all the days her ex could choose to call, it had to be this day, at this time. She really did have all the luck, didn't she.

"I'm only going to ask this one more time, then I'm going to hang up. What do you want?"

"Fine," he said, no longer laughing. *"I'm calling with good news, actually. Are you sitting down?"*

"Patrick." Her tone conveyed her warning. He was on thin ice, and she didn't care how good he claimed this news was—she was in no mood for games.

"Okay, fine, you're really killing the vibe, Tess, but here goes. I got your job back for you! You start the day after Christmas, so all you have to do is get here by then."

Tess sucked in a breath, completely caught off guard by his news. Then a thought occurred that had her questioning everything.

"If you really got my job back, why didn't my old boss call to tell me himself?" She never suspected Patrick of being cruel, but then again, what was ghosting her in her time of need if not cruel?

"Wow, I thought you'd be happy," he said angrily. *"I never expected the third degree, but since you're so suspicious these days, I asked Rob if I could be the one to call you. I never*

stopped caring about you, Tess, I just needed time to sort things out."

Is that what they were calling it these days? Even if what he was saying was true, he could have told her that at any time. Then again, now that she'd torpedoed any chance she had with Molly, did she have a choice other than to return to Chicago?

"I—I need to think about this," she told him. "Even if I can get there by Tuesday morning, there's still the problem of where I'll live." Not only that, this would force her to travel on Christmas, and then there was the little problem of them firing her again. If they were willing to fire her once, who's to say they wouldn't do it a second time? Maybe it was time to consider a career change?

"You can stay with me," he offered, though his voice lacked the warmth such an invitation should invoke. *"Look Tess, I really went out on a limb for you, okay? Don't make me look bad by flaking on me. Tuesday morning, eight o'clock sharp. Got it?"*

"I got it," she replied, her mind elsewhere. At some point, he must have hung up, because when she checked her phone, the call had ended.

What should she do? Aunt Bea would give her the money to get there, but did she really want to go back? There was no way she could ever trust Patrick again, so living with him was out of the question. So that left her without a place to stay. Then there was the issue with the job itself, which she still wasn't sure was legit. But even if it was, how long would it be before another round of layoffs occurred? And why would she assume she wouldn't be one of the first to go, just like last time?

The answer seemed clear, and yet, she still wasn't sure what to do. If she changed careers, what then? This was too much to work through in a parking lot. It was time to go home and put together a pros and cons list. Only then could she make sense of things and find a clear path forward.

At least she hoped that's what would happen.

Chapter 15

Tess spent half of Friday night making list after list, but there was no winner—neither pro nor con—to be found. She'd planned to try again Saturday night, but the day had been so chaotic that by the time she got home, she'd fallen into bed and immediately passed out. And now it was Sunday, the day before Christmas, the day when she absolutely *had* to make a decision about Chicago if she were to leave the following day. And yet, she still didn't have an answer.

"Hey Aunt Bea," she said as she slowly made her way to the coffee pot. She poured the biggest cup she could find, savoring the aromatic smell as she waited for it to cool enough to take her first drink.

"You look terrible," Bea replied, her eyes narrowed as she studied Tess. "Is that because you worked your tail off yesterday? Or is something else going on?"

How did one answer that when they'd literally destroyed their life? *Should* she answer that? At some point Bea would ask about the interviews Tess had told her about, but did she really need to get into it now? "I guess I'm not used to that level of physical activity," she said, doing her best impression of a woman smiling.

It was clear from the look on her face Bea did not believe her, but she mercifully decided to let it go.

"You should take a nap after church," Bea finally replied. "That should help."

Tess's eyes widened at the mention of church. The same church Molly and Grant attended. The same church Tess would no doubt run into Molly and Grant should she go today. She liked to think of herself as a strong woman, but this was a bridge too far. No way did she have the courage to face them again after the way she acted Friday. "I'm really not feeling well," Tess lied. "I think it would be best if I stayed home. I don't want to risk getting someone sick right before Christmas."

Bea crossed the room and placed the back of her hand against Tess's forehead. "You don't seem to be running a fever," she said, pulling her hand back. "C'mon Tess, you don't want to miss church on today of all days, do you?"

Yes, she absolutely *did* want to do that, but there was no way she could get out of this without upsetting Bea—and likely Junior as well—so she sighed and gave in. "I'll go get ready," she muttered.

When they pulled up to the church, the parking lot was overflowing with vehicles. Since it hadn't been like that the last two Sundays, Tess could only assume people were there for the Christmas service. As they walked up to the entrance, Tess kept an eye out for Molly and Grant. If only she had a hat she could use to cover her face. Women used to wear hats to church—who decided that should go out of fashion? Must have been people who didn't have a habit of sticking their foot in their mouth every time they opened it.

For once in her life, lady luck was on her side. The church was so packed, they were forced to take seats in the back, as opposed to their usual seats near the front. That significantly improved her odds of getting out of there without being seen. Her mood slightly improved, Tess laser-focused on Pastor Steve. She was so intent on watching him, she failed to notice Austin slide into the pew next to her until his arm had casually draped around her shoulders.

Surprised, she looked at him, taking in his dress shirt, slacks, and formal boots. He really was a handsome man, and that was before he gave her that lopsided grin of his. "What are you doing here?" she whispered. "I thought you had to work?"

Bea leaned forward, curious as who Tess was talking to. When she saw it was Austin, and waved hello. He waved back, then nodded at Junior, who grunted in response.

Austin turned his attention back to Tess. "It's Christmas Eve," he whispered. When she stared at him blankly, he shook his head. "I took the day off, duh!" he teased.

That was good enough for her. She snuggled closer, then leaned her head against his shoulder, trusting him to nudge her should she accidentally fall asleep. As Pastor Steve talked about gold, frankincense, and myrrh, Tess sat up straight, her eyes wild with panic. She still hadn't bought Christmas presents! Were there any stores open on

Christmas Eve? Luckily, she only had three people to shop for, but that didn't matter if all the stores were closed.

"What's wrong?" Austin whispered in her ear.

Tess shook her head, unwilling to risk Bea's wrath by getting caught talking during the sermon. She would just have to borrow her aunt's car and drive from store to store until she found one that was open. Either that, or get everyone snacks from the gas station. Maybe she could throw in a couple of gift cards for gas? Perhaps a stale taquito that had been spinning on that warming machine for the last couple of days? Wouldn't that be a fine gift to give her loved ones, especially if it was before she said goodbye again.

Now that she had some semblance of a plan, she settled down, her head once again leaning against Austin. She was tempted to invite him to go shopping with her, but since he was one of the few she needed a gift for, that seemed impractical. What should she get him, anyway? Better to save that little conundrum until she found a store; options were sure to be limited, and well, beggars can't be choosers.

As Pastor Steve began to wrap up his sermon, the church pianist returned to the piano. It was time to plan her getaway, which would now be made all the more difficult since Austin was with her. She glanced around the church, careful not to make eye contact with anyone, until she spotted Molly. To her chagrin, she was also seated in the back, two sections over. That left two choices: either she stays where she is and looks heavily involved in conversation with someone until Molly left, or she should immediately bolt out of the church the second the prayer was over.

When Pastor Steve said amen, the congregation rose as a whole and began to file into the aisles, leaving Tess trapped. Looks like it was option two. She quickly turned her back toward the section Molly was in and began to speak to Austin in earnest. "Do you see where Molly and Grant are sitting?" she asked in a hushed tone.

Austin looked over her shoulder, then nodded. "Do you want me to help you get to her?"

"What?" Tess asked in surprise. "No, not at all. I want you to tell me when she leaves."

"Okayyy," he drawled. "Why are we hiding from Molly?"

Why was everyone so nosy? "Can you just trust me on this, please?"

He gave her a strange look, then shrugged. "Would you like to have lunch with me?"

This wasn't the ideal situation, but it would work. "Yes, but I need to go to the city for some last-minute shopping. Any chance you can take me there?"

"Sure," he bumped her shoulder playfully. "Is this, like, our first real date?"

Tess bit back a groan. How was she supposed to answer that? Obviously she would love to say yes, but there was still the possibility she was about to leave. She would have to explain all that eventually—might as well do it on the way.

"It doesn't have to be," he said, his smile fading.

"No, it's not that," she said, quick to assure him. "I'll explain in the truck. Is it safe to leave yet?"

Austin looked over her shoulder again. "She's still here, but the aisle has cleared if you want to make a run for it."

She chanced a glance in Molly's direction, saw she was busy getting the baby in her car seat, then turned back to Austin and nodded. "Let's do it."

They hustled out of church, then ran to his truck, smiling and laughing all the way. Once they were safely inside, Austin leaned over and kissed her.

"You need to laugh like that more," he said, gently stroking her hair.

"I agree," she replied, staring up into his eyes. She honestly couldn't remember the last time she'd felt that carefree, even if it was only for a moment. "We should get out of here."

He continued to play with her hair, in no hurry to leave. "Want to tell me what all the fuss is about?"

No, she still didn't want to do that, but if she had to, she might as well get it over with. "I'll tell you once you get on the road," she said, stalling as long as she could. Once she spilled her guts, Austin would never look at her the same again.

Austin did as he was told, even waiting until they'd left town to prompt her a third time. "Well?"

Tess sighed, then recounted every gory detail of her exchange with Molly. When she was finished, she sat back and waited for the judgment that was sure to come.

"Wow," Austin said, letting out a low whistle. "You really let her have it, didn't you?"

"Um," Tess looked at him out of the corner of her eye. "Yes, but I feel like you're missing the part where she now hates me and wants nothing to do with me."

He reached over and took her hand. "Nah, Molly's not one to hold a grudge. I'm sure she'll come around once she's had a chance to recover from the shock of your epic rant!"

Tess playfully smacked his arm. "This is serious! Not only did I insult her, I ruined my entire career." She sighed again. "And that's not all that happened." She told him about the call from Patrick and how he offered her her job back.

"Is that what you want?" he asked once she'd finished spilling her guts. He kept his eyes on the road, his posture stiff as he waited for her reply.

"No," Tess admitted without hesitation. "But I don't know what else to do."

Austin pulled into the parking lot of a small, family-owned Mexican restaurant, parked the truck, then turned to face her. He took her hands in his, gently rubbing them with his thumbs. "When you first left Winterwood, you were running away from something. When you came back, you were running away from something. If you leave again... are you sensing a pattern?"

"Each time I thought it was the opposite, and that I was running to something, not away," she argued. "I still believe that wanting to live in the city does not make me a bad person."

"No one ever said it did," he reminded her. "It's you who said that, every single time, Tess. But this isn't a question of whether or not you're a bad person—the only question here is, what would make you happy?"

It sounded so simple when he said it, but she knew it wasn't. "If I don't go, how will I support myself? Even if I stay on at the bakery, or get a job at the grocery store, or some other minimum wage job, I won't make enough to pay back my loans *and* pay for rent, utilities, and food. I can't live with my aunt and uncle forever; that's too much of a burden on them."

"You could always start your own marketing agency," he suggested. "It worked for Molly, so there's no reason it shouldn't work for you. Or, if you're set on starting a new career, I'm sure Bea and Junior would be happy for you to live with them while you went back to school for a year or two." He lifted her face with his finger. "The point is, you have options that don't include moving in with your shady ex."

He had a point, and once she realized that, she felt a weight lift off her shoulders. "You're right," she said, smiling up at him. "I do have options, and it's time I start planning for the future I want, not the one I feel forced into."

"Glad you're finally listening to me," he teased. "Now let's go eat, I'm starving!"

Tess laughed, then followed him into the restaurant. Now all she had to do was find three cheap, yet meaningful, gifts and all her problems would be solved! If only it were that easy.

Chapter 16

Merry Christmas!

The big day had finally arrived, though Tess hadn't realized she was counting down to it until now. More stores had been open the day before than expected, so she'd thankfully been able to find the gifts she needed. Even though her days of waking up early to see what 'Santa' brought were over, she was still looking forward to their holiday gathering—especially since Austin was joining them.

Speaking of Austin, they'd spent the previous evening at the high school watching the drama club put on a humorous rendition of *A Christmas Carol*. She wasn't certain it was *supposed* to be humorous, but the cast had done such an amazing job, she was proud of them regardless. The part that had been difficult was discovering Molly was also there, along with Grant, Emilio, and Vanessa. Despite her best efforts, she'd run into them on her way out of the building, and while their interaction had been pleasant, there was still an undercurrent of unease coursing through it. Tess had apologized again, profusely, but had a feeling things would continue to be awkward for the foreseeable future.

"Merry Christmas!" she said to Bea as she entered the kitchen. "Where's Uncle Junior?"

Bea took a sip from her coffee cup, then set aside the crossword puzzle she was working on. "He's out doing the morning chores," she replied. "The animals don't care it's a holiday!"

Tess should have realized that, but she decided to give herself some grace this morning. "When do you want to get started on the turkey?"

"In about thirty minutes," Bea said, checking her watch.

That would give her plenty of time to talk to Bea. She just hoped she didn't ruin Christmas with her request. Tess grabbed her coffee and sat down opposite Bea. "I've decided to stay in Winterwood," she announced. She then held her breath while she waited for Bea's reaction.

"Do you have a plan?" Bea asked, her face unreadable.

While she hadn't expected Bea to do cartwheels around the kitchen, Tess had hoped for at least a little positivity. Had she seriously misjudged her aunt's feelings? Was Bea anxious for her to leave? Now that all these doubts had entered her mind, she was reluctant to continue the conversation. "Yes, but maybe we should do this another time..." She grabbed her coffee and pushed her chair back. She was about to stand when Bea reached across the table and laid her hand on Tess's arm.

"There's no need to run off," she told her. "Your uncle and I are happy to have you here. I just want to know if you're finally following your heart, or if this is another attempt to avoid making hard decisions?"

Tess scooted her chair back to the table, then took a long sip of coffee as she gathered her thoughts. "Choosing to stay feels like the hard decision," she said with a wry laugh. "But it's the only decision that feels right." At least for now, but she decided to leave that part out.

"In that case, I'm thrilled to hear that!" Bea said enthusiastically. "I'm sure Austin will be as well!"

That much was true—Austin had been pretty happy when she'd made the decision the day before. Now with that out of the way comes the hard part. "There's still the matter of work," she began, but Bea waved her off.

"Let's save all that for another day," she said. "Today is a day for celebration! And I, for one, am thankful you're here to celebrate with us." She smiled wistfully. "It's been a long time since we had family here for the holidays. Who knows, by this time next year we could have a little one with us!"

Tess's eyes widened like saucers. "Aunt Bea!" she exclaimed. "Austin and I have just started dating! A year is a bit unrealistic for something like that."

Bea shrugged. "Fine, have it your way. Two years, then!"

They laughed, Tess shaking her head in disbelief. It wasn't that long ago she'd believed her future lay with another man. While Austin was definitely nothing like Patrick, who's to say they'd get married and have kids? She still needed to get her life together, but a part of her didn't hate the idea. Nor was it hard to imagine a couple of little kids chasing each other around the kitchen table while she and Aunt Bea got Christmas dinner ready.

"I can tell by the dreamy look on your face you're considering it," Bea teased. She stood up and walked to the kitchen sink, depositing her cup in one side, then draining the other side where the turkey had been defrosting in water. "You ready to get this bad boy in the oven?" she asked over her shoulder.

Tess was more than ready. This would be her first home-cooked holiday meal in years. When she lived in Chicago, she and her friends always went to a Chinese restaurant on Christmas. She'd thought she was 'trendy' and 'hip,' and while she didn't regret it, a part of her had longed for home at the same time; she just hadn't been willing to admit it. "I'm ready!" she replied enthusiastically. She hopped out of her seat and joined Bea by the sink. It was like old times again, and she couldn't be happier.

***

Christmas music played softly in the background, lights twinkled brightly on the tree, while the smell of turkey and freshly baked pies swirled around them mixed with the scent of pine and caramel apple cider. The table was decorated with candles mixed with poinsettias and holly, the 'good' china laid out in front of four chairs. As Tess stepped back to admire her work, a smile lit up her face. Maybe she should pursue a career in interior design—it certainly sounded fun!

Ding Dong

"I'll get it," she called out. "It's probably Austin."

Sure enough, when she opened the door, Austin was waiting on the other side.

"I brought you something," he said, a mischievous smile on his face.

"Oh yeah? What's that?"

He pulled his hand from behind his back and handed her the reindeer headband. "Merry Christmas!"

Tess laughed as she accepted the headband. "Merry Christmas!" she said, putting it on her head. "How do I look?" She struck a pose, then burst into laughter.

They went inside and took their seats at the table.

"It's good to see you again," Bea said to Austin.

He smiled and nodded politely.

"I just saw you yesterday," Junior grumbled.

Austin grinned and patted him on the back. "It's nice to see you, too!"

Conversation turned to Bea's retirement as they passed bowls of stuffing, green beans, mashed potatoes, and gravy around the table.

"What do you think you'll do once it's official?" Austin asked.

Bea's smile faded a bit. "Well, I was hoping Junior and I might finally get to travel, but someone isn't ready to join me in retirement, so..."

Junior coughed, then covered his mouth with a napkin. "Let's not ruin a perfectly good meal, okay? I told you we can travel—I just need to find someone to take over farm duties while we're gone." He gave Austin the side-eye. "Perhaps that someone is closer than we think."

Tess wasn't sure what to make of all this, but felt compelled to step in before Austin got dragged into something he might not want. "What do we have planned at the bakery this week? Should I expect another week of chaos, or will we get a bit of a reprieve now that Christmas is over?"

"Chaos!" all three of them answered at once.

"What do y'all know that I don't?" Tess asked with a groan. She was tempted to lay her head against the table but didn't want to risk getting gravy on her reindeer antlers. No wonder her aunt was ready to retire—Tess had only been at it two weeks and she was ready to retire too!

Bea's smile widened as she perked up. "We are catering the dessert portion of a large anniversary party on New Year's Eve!" she said with excitement. "Then there's the orders we get for people's regular parties, and on top of that, Grace is opening the hotel for the week and typically orders doughnuts and pastries at least a few times."

"Should be an interesting week," Tess said weakly. "I really hope Jenny shows up."

"You and me both," Bea replied.

Dinner was just about done, so they sent the men to the living room while Bea and Tess put the food up and did a cursory cleaning, opting to wash the dishes later.

"Okay, everyone, present time!" Tess announced as they joined the men. She walked to the tree and grabbed the boxes she'd wrapped the night before, then handed one to each of them.

"Oh, honey, you shouldn't have!" Bea said as she accepted hers. It was rather large, but when she shook it, it didn't make a sound. "I guess I'll go first," she said as everyone watched.

Bea carefully peeled back the wrapping paper to reveal a brown box. When she struggled to remove the tape, Junior pulled a knife out of his back pocket and handed it to her. "Oh wow," she gushed as she revealed the contents of the box. She held up each item as she pulled it out: a fluffy bathrobe, slippers, a foot bath, neck massager, and bath salts. "Why, it's a spa kit!"

Tess watched her expression to see if she liked it, pleased to see that she did. "I thought you could use some pampering after a long day at the bakery!" She turned to her uncle. "Your turn, Uncle Junior!"

Junior took his knife back from Bea, then made short work of opening his box. He then pulled the items out, much like Bea did: a farmer's almanac, cooling towels, rechargeable hand warmers, and a pair of fancy gloves. "Thank you," he said, nodding when he was finished.

He was a hard man to read, but Tess was fairly confident he liked his gift. She supposed time would tell, but if she noticed him using even one of the items over the next few days, she'd consider her gift a success.

Now it was Austin's turn, and her nerves began to get the better of her. While it was true they'd known each other most of their lives, it had been years since they'd connected. In fact, they'd spent almost all of their adult lives apart. Did he still like the same things he used to? She supposed she was about to find out.

Austin pulled out his own knife and opened his box. He looked inside, raised his brow, then looked at Tess before pulling items out one by one: a 'kiss the cook' apron, BBQ seasoning gift set, and a box of baking soda. He held up the last one and grinned. "Really?"

"Just in case," she teased.

Bea exchanged a glance with Junior. "I feel like we're missing something here."

"Oven fire," Tess said—no further explanation necessary.

"Ah, I see," Bea nodded. She grabbed a small box and handed it to Tess. "This one's for you."

Touched they thought of her, Tess accepted the gift, then gently removed the wrapping to reveal a jewelry box. When she lifted the lid, she discovered a key nestled in the velvet.

"It's a key to the house," Bea explained. "We wanted to make it official by giving you your own key."

Tess blinked back tears as she hugged Bea. "Thank you," she said, her voice hoarse with emotion. She knew in her heart the real gift wasn't the key, or even them allowing her to stay—it was forgiveness, and that meant more to her than anything else ever could.

She took a deep breath, then faced her uncle. "Are you really okay with this?"

Junior waved her over, then gave her a bear hug. "Of course I am," he said gruffly. "I've always loved you, sweetheart, even when I didn't like the choices you made."

Now that she'd officially made peace with Junior, the final weight lifted from her shoulders.

They exchanged a few more gifts, then Bea and Junior excused themselves.

"How about we go for a walk?" Austin asked, holding out his hand.

"I'd love to," she said, placing her hand in his.

They went outside, Austin momentarily stopping by his truck before leading her out to one of the fields. "Remember when we used to play out here as kids?"

She squeezed his hand and smiled. "You were a dashing cowboy to my barrel racer!"

"And look at us now!" he teased. He stopped by a tree and leaned against it. "Things were a lot simpler back then, weren't they?"

Why did that sound like the beginning of a breakup conversation? "I guess," she hesitated to reply, unsure of how to respond.

Austin pulled a box out of his pocket and handed it to her.

Confused, Tess accepted it, then gasped when she lifted the lid. Inside was a gorgeous opal ring, the white stone shimmering in the light.

"It belonged to my mother," he said softly. "We are a long way from a marriage proposal, but I wanted to make sure my intentions are clear." He took the ring out of the box and slipped it on her ring finger. "I've loved you since we were teenagers, Tess. I knew I needed to let you go, but I've always prayed that if we were meant to be, you'd find your way back to me. And now that you have, I have zero desire to let you go again."

Too choked up to speak, Tess threw her arms around him and hugged him tight. "That sounds good to me," she whispered. "But don't tell Bea—she's already dreaming of babies by next Christmas!"

"And what are you dreaming of?" he whispered, his finger gently tracing her jawline.

"I'm dreaming of... mistletoe?" She looked up and saw the telltale leaves and berries of the famous plant hanging from a branch. "What's that?" she asked, pointing to the branch.

Austin looked up and grinned. "That?" he asked. "I believe you already know what that is. Fancy finding that here..."

Tess rolled her eyes. "You goofball! You don't need mistletoe to get me to kiss you!"

He pulled her close, then looked deep into her eyes. "I didn't want to take any chances," he said as his head lowered to hers.

"Merry Christmas!" Tess said against his lips.

"Merry Christmas!"

Epilogue

Tess was hard at work the next morning when her phone rang. She checked her watch and smiled: nine o'clock on the dot. Instead of answering, she let it go to voicemail, then blocked the number.

Just for fun, she decided to listen to the message:

**Heavy breathing* "You had better be stuck in traffic, Tess. I'm serious, you have no idea how bad I look right now." *More breathing* "Please just give me a call and let me know you're on your way, okay?"*

She put her phone back in her pocket, then went back to dusting sugar on the freshly baked doughnuts. Part of her felt bad—if that message was real, and not some sort of prank like she suspected—then he had attempted to help her out by getting her job back. On the other hand, if the only time he was willing to talk to her was when they were employed at the same company, well, that's just weird. She almost felt like her work had been part of a cult or something.

To put her mind at ease, she decided to call her old boss and simply ask him if what Patrick had said was true.

Ring Ring

"Rob speaking, how may I help you?"

"Hi Rob, it's Tess." She took a deep breath, then got straight to the point. "Patrick called me last Friday and said you were willing to give me my job back. Since you'd already told me that was out of your hands, I just thought I'd check in with you before I made any plans."

"What!" Rob sputtered. *"I'm sorry, Tess, but that did not happen. We would never make an offer of employment through another employee; that is simply unprofessional."* He paused for a moment, the sound of keys clacking on a keyboard coming over the speaker. *"I hope you're doing well, but I'm afraid there will be no further opportunities with this company, now or in the future."*

That was just as she suspected. She now had a new nickname for Patrick: Pat the Rat! But oh well, she'd had no intention of going back anyway, so no harm, no foul. "Thank you, Rob, I hope you had a Merry Christmas, and wish you a Happy New Year!"

"Um, same to you," he said, surprised by her kind message.

Tess hung up, then returned to her doughnuts. She briefly wondered what sort of scheme Patrick had cooked up—as well as why he would do such a cruel thing—then decided he wasn't worth her time and energy. Some people were just mean. Maybe someone hurt him in the past? Maybe this was some lame attempt at generating street cred among the other employees. Whatever it was, it was no longer her problem, and she intended to keep it that way.

Ring Ring

Assuming it was Patrick again, calling from a different number, Tess allowed the call to go to voicemail again.

Ring Ring

Certainly, he didn't plan to spend the day calling her from different numbers?

Ring Ring

That was it! She was willing to let it go, but now she was going to give that guy a piece of her mind!

When she checked the caller ID, she saw Molly's name on the screen and quickly answered.

"Hello," she said hesitantly.

"Hey Tess, is there any way you can go to my office?"

Tess grimaced. It was more than likely Molly wanted to tell her the two interviews were off, as if Tess hadn't already expected that. She was tempted to tell her that over the phone and spare them both the awkwardness of that conversation, but figured she might as well accept another opportunity to apologize. "I'll be there in a few minutes."

Once she hung up, she checked her call logs, and sure enough, the last two calls had been from Chicago numbers. She had a feeling the only reason the calls stopped was due to Rob calling Patrick into his office to ream him out. Oh well, time to forget about that and face the music—again.

She informed Bea where she was going, then headed to Molly's office, her trepidation growing the closer she got.

When Tess walked into the building, the first thing she noticed was how quiet it was—which was odd since she'd been asked to come. Was Molly pranking her too? She headed straight for Molly's office, her concern growing when it was empty.

Ring Ring

Tess looked down at her phone and saw Molly's name. Great, this was also a prank.

She blinked a couple of times to clear her mind, then answered. "Look Molly, I cannot apologize enough for my actions the other day. I am truly sorry, but I don't think I deserve whatever this is. I can assure you, I understand the interviews are off, so I'm just going to see myself out, okay?"

"Wait," Molly said, a tinge of panic in her voice. *"That's not why I asked you to go to my office."*

Tess sat down, thoroughly intrigued. And if she were honest, a little scared. What more did Molly want from her? What more could she give?

"I would have rather done this in person, but Eliza is sick, so we are holed up at home until she gets better. That's why you're there."

"I'm afraid I don't understand," Tess said, her eyes narrowed in confusion.

Molly sighed as the sound of a baby fussing could be heard over the phone. *"I don't have much time. My daughter needs me, and so do my clients. Since I can't take care of both at the same time, I need you to fill in for me. Consider this a probation period. If you knock this out of the park, I'll hire you on full-time."*

"But what about Friday?" Tess asked, unable to process what she was hearing.

"I've been doing a lot of thinking over the last few days, and while I wasn't thrilled with your accusations, I do appreciate the boldness with which you made them. We need people who are willing to speak up when they see injustice—but those people need to be sure actual injustice is occurring, you know what I mean?"

"Of course," Tess said quickly. "I completely agree. My actions were rash, and honestly, highly influenced by negative experiences over the years. I need to do better at making sure I have the whole story first."

"Good, I'm glad we agree. Not to be rude, but do you want the job or not?"

"Oh!" Tess said, her mouth opening in surprise. "Yes, of course I want the job. What do you need me to do?"

Molly breathed a sigh of relief. *"As soon as we hang up, I'll call Emilio and ask him to set you up with a computer and access to my files. While he's doing that, I'll send you a detailed email of what I need you to do."*

"That sounds perfect!" Tess said enthusiastically. She looked down at her icing-streaked clothes and winced. "I'm not exactly dressed for this."

"Don't worry about that for today. I'm sure you'll need to talk to Bea and perhaps finish a few tasks at the bakery, but if you're able to start this afternoon, that would be awesome."

Tess pumped her fist in glee. "This afternoon is perfect. I'll be here at one, if that's okay?"

"Thank you, Tess, I'm really looking forward to working with you. In all honesty, I should have hired someone a long time ago. Guess I was just waiting for the right person!"

That was high praise coming from someone like Molly, especially after the way Tess had behaved. She checked her watch—only three hours until Molly wanted her to start. That didn't give her a lot of time, but she'd make it work.

Back at the bakery, she found Bea in the kitchen icing cookies. "You'll never guess what just happened!" she exclaimed.

Bea looked up, her brow raised. "I did happen to notice a ring on *that* particular finger," she stated. "Am I closer to getting grandbabies than I thought?"

Tess smiled at the thought of Bea and Junior filling grandparent roles with her future children. Lord knows they'd filled the parental role with her more than her own parents ever had. "Not yet," she said quickly. "Molly just hired me!"

"That's wonderful news!" Bea said, setting the icing down and coming around the counter to hug Tess. "Didn't I tell you things would work out?"

"Yes, you did!" Tess said with a laugh. "I should have listened to you, but it's hard when things seem hopeless."

"Things are never hopeless, child," Bea replied, giving her another hug. "When does she want you to start?"

Leaving Bea to run the bakery alone seemed cruel after everything Bea had done for her, but she didn't know what else to do. "This afternoon," Tess winced. "But I have enough time to finish my tasks before I go, and then I can come in early and stay late the rest of the week."

"Don't worry about that," Bea told her. "Jenny showed up today, and according to her, plans to be here the rest of the week. You go focus on your new job. And man," she teased.

"Thank you, Aunt Bea," Tess said, giving her one more hug. "For everything," she whispered.

Tess left the bakery feeling like a new woman. She had a new job, a new place to live, and she'd reconnected with her first love. The cherry on top of the cake was reuniting with her family. It would take some time, and effort on her part, but before long, she hoped to also reunite with her old friends. Grace had been right—this truly was the season of miracles.

Afterword

Dear Reader,

Thank you so much for reading *Dreaming of Mistletoe*! I had so much fun writing this book, and I really hope you liked reading it just as much! Christmas is my absolute favorite time of the year, so after I finished *Countdown to a Wedding*, I just had to write another Christmas book! The only problem was, there are already two Christmas books in the Holiday Countdown Series, so I had to get creative! I hope you enjoyed meeting Tess and Austin; I love expanding the town and showcasing other characters—not to mention, it was a blast including all the Easter eggs. There will be more Countdown books, but more spin-offs are coming as well!

If this is the first book of mine you've read, and you want to read more, *Countdown to Christmas* is the first book in the Holiday Countdown Series, and there are currently nine more books after that!

I am so thankful to everyone who reads my books. I know you literally have millions of other options, so it means the world to me that you chose to read mine! I would also like to give a little shout-out to my youngest fan, JT, as well as to his amazing grandmother, Tammy! It's not often authors get a chance to get to know our readers, but I have loved getting to know them!

If you would like to say hello, receive news about new releases, and other announcements, you can join my newsletter at diannahouxshop.com

I wish you all a very Merry Christmas, a Happy New Year, or, if you prefer, Happy Holidays!

-Dianna Houx

www.ingramcontent.com/pod-product-compliance
Lightning Source LLC
LaVergne TN
LVHW091048150826
845673LV00002B/505

* 9 7 8 1 9 6 3 0 8 7 1 8 5 *